The Book of the Staff

Also by Eric R. Asher

Keep track of Eric's new releases by receiving an email on release day. It's fast and easy to sign up for Eric's mailing list, and you'll also get an ebook copy of the subscriber exclusive anthology, *Whispers of War*.

Go here to get started: www.ericrasher.com

The Steamborn Trilogy:

Steamborn
Steamforged
Steamsworn

The Vesik Series:
(Recommended for Ages 17+)

Days Gone Bad
Wolves and the River of Stone
Winter's Demon
This Broken World
Destroyer Rising
Rattle the Bones
Witch Queen's War
Forgotten Ghosts
The Book of the Ghost
The Book of the Claw
The Book of the Sea
The Book of the Staff
The Book of the Rune*

The Book of the Sails*
The Book of the Wing*
The Book of the Blade*
The Book of the Fang*
The Book of the Reaper*

The Vesik Series Box Sets

Box Set One (Books 1-3)
Box Set Two (Books 4-6)
Box Set Three (Books 7-8)
Box Set Four: The Books of the Dead Part 1 (Coming in 2020)*
Box Set Five: The Books of the Dead Part 2 (Coming in 2020)*

Mason Dixon – Monster Hunter:

Episode One
Episode Two
Episode Three

*Want to receive an email when one of Eric's books releases? Sign up for Eric's mailing list.
www.ericrasher.com

The Book of
the Staff

Eric R. Asher

Edited by Laura Matheson
Cover typography by Indie Solutions by Murphy Rae
Cover design ©Phatpuppyart.com – Claudia McKinney

Things forgotten will always return.

CHAPTER ONE

KODA WALKED THROUGH the ancient stone hallway, ghostly torches casting as much shadow as they did light. It was a place he'd been far more times than he could recall, but rarely had the hour felt so late, or the stakes so high.

Pieces of the conversation he'd had with the elders of the Society of Flame echoed through his mind. Was there something more he could have said? To help them understand better?

Koda rolled his oversized prayer beads between his fingers. The old stones had been given to him almost a decade before he died. He'd been surprised to find they still felt as though they had physical weight.

Now, centuries after joining the Society of Flame, conserving their secrets, and bestowing knowledge upon leaders who would shape the world, his own council of elders were failing him. None of them had taken the time to speak with Damian since it was clear he was a mantle bearer.

And now … in the most unlikely of times, an ally he hadn't expected. What did a mage solis have to offer a trapped god?

The panda bear padding along beside Koda chuffed.

"Did I say that out loud?" Koda asked, patting the bear on the head out of habit more than an actual belief the old samurai wanted head scratches.

The light of the torches changed, took on the orange glow of living flame as the pair crossed the sanctum. A world between worlds was where the Society of Flame lived, and if they didn't change their ways, it was where they'd perish as they placed the value of their archives above the lives of those they could aid.

Happy changed as they exited the sanctum, his form narrowing into hunched shoulders until the stride of a quadruped became the rigid posture of an armored man.

He looked to Shiawase. "You once told me you could fight better as a bear."

"That may be true in many cases, but it is a great deal harder to whisper."

Koda inclined his head and led the way around a corner built from sheer gray stone. It wasn't perfect like the sanctum had been. This place showed its age, and as the corridor opened before them, it revealed a multi-tiered castle filled with ageless doorways.

"It never ceases to impress," Shiawase said, his gaze trailing up the tower of doors.

"It is hard to imagine what power could have built it, or how many organizations have dwelled inside its great halls."

"Cults," Shiawase said. "I believe the word you're looking for is cults."

Koda inclined his head. This place had been home to more than one *cult*. He didn't like that word much, as some of those close-knit groups had made great progress in the art of wards and conservation before they were destroyed by the Watchers.

"Perhaps they will call the Society of Flame a cult one day," Koda said, leading the way to a wide spiral staircase.

They followed the curve of the bronze railing, rich with Celtic knots and wards of its own. Neither of them made a sound as Koda's robes and Shiawase's armor whispered in the silence.

On the second floor, they passed a bright green door that looked as though it had been freshly painted. An intricate ruin of scorch marks marred the door beside it. They walked past a simple black door with an old silver lock before Koda slowed. The fourth was red stone like the body of the Old God called Aeros.

Koda stopped there and exchanged a glance with Shiawase. "You need not make this journey, my friend."

"I've been dead a long time, Koda. If this is the end, I'll embrace it gladly for Vicky."

Koda gave Shiawase a shallow bow before twisting the cold stone doorknob and stepping into a brilliant blue light.

This was not the Warded Ways. Not the chaos of the Abyss. An ocean of magic surrounded them, pure and brilliant and welcoming. This place, the road between realms as the Fae once called it, was something else. Lost magic to all but a few.

But that brilliant light didn't last. One step in, and one step out. Koda sighed as the last of the light faded and they left the ocean of magic behind.

"It is a shame we cannot spend more time in that place," Shiawase said. "It is a rare thing to feel such peace. I do not understand it."

Trees took shape around them, shadowed by the late morning sun. Long-abandoned train tracks peeked out from the covering of fallen leaves and detritus of the forest floor.

To the side were the stone remains of a train station that once carried quarried stone far from where they now stood. Old bricks still stood on three sides, but as Koda turned toward the vanished wall, he saw the silhouette.

Golden armor glinted in the sun, almost blinding to look upon, as it had likely been designed a great many years ago. The man eyed them, his short black hair standing still against the breeze rustling the dead leaves around them.

Shiawase's hand rested on the hilt of his sword.

"You kept your word," Koda said. It wasn't an accusation, more an acknowledgment that the Watcher hadn't burned them to ash the moment they stepped from the gateway.

Edgar—Watcher, mage solis, immortal—smiled. "Did I not tell you the council would remain neutral?"

Koda twisted the prayer beads between his fingers before letting them fall back against his pale gray cloak. "Some days, I do not think they deserve the title, but I am not ready to give up on them. I did hope you would be mistaken."

Edgar nodded. "To a degree, I was. But that would be considered cheating."

Shiawase frowned at Edgar's somewhat cryptic words and stepped closer. "You would play games, at a time like this?"

Edgar reached up as if to adjust the bowler hat he

wasn't wearing. It was odd to see the immortal without it. "Not games, Shiawase. Not games at all. There's more than one database that remains of the Watchers' knowledge. I simply found what we need."

"A new anchor for the devil's knot?" Koda asked. "Truly?"

"A theory, at least," Edgar said. "One of the archives of the mage machina documented a story from a time around the Revolutionary War. A woman, gifted much as our friend Ward, tried many different anchors to save more than one life. What she learned after a great many … experiments, was that the devil's knot cannot be anchored to an inanimate object. It must be anchored to a soul."

Shiawase sighed at those words, shoulders slumping a hair. "That leaves us back where we started."

Edgar rubbed the back of his hand beneath his gauntlet. "Of course, a soul doesn't have to be in a body."

Shiawase froze.

Koda stood up straighter. "What are you saying? We could use a ghost as an anchor?"

"Not any ghost," Edgar said. "And you need more than just the ghost themselves."

"A binding," Koda said, his voice trailing off as the wheels started to spin in his mind. "You're talking about a binding ward to tie a soul and a devil's knot together. To anchor it to something using a soulart." Koda raised his eyes to look upon Edgar. "You speak of treasonous arts, friend."

"I once believed that," Edgar said. "And perhaps there was some logic to it, given how dangerous the outcome has been. But that boy has saved far more lives than he's hurt. And he did it with magicks that have been forbidden longer than we've lived upon this rock."

"It is how the magic is wielded that defines it," Shiawase said. "But any art so dangerous could bring ruin upon those who wield it and those who are in its way."

Edgar grimaced. "You might not like my suggestion, Shiawase. But it's for Vicky. Remember that."

Koda turned to gaze at the samurai, suspicion of Edgar's plan already forming on his lips. "You wish to bind him to the girl. To use Shiawase as the anchor for the devil's knot. Have you gone mad?"

"We cannot lose the girl," Edgar said, his words hurried. "If we lose her, we lose Damian. We lose Sam. We lose the fraying threads of what's holding our damned army together."

"And perhaps the most dangerous creature ever to set foot upon this earth will perish," Koda said, though the words felt wrong. "There is much to consider, I do not know how—"

"I'll do it," Shiawase said, his fingers flexing around the hilt of his sheathed sword.

"We do not know the risks!" Koda said, snapping his arm out in a violent gesture to Shiawase. "You could be sacrificing yourself for nothing."

"I could be sacrificing myself for that child. For that one light left to burn away the shadows. It is worth the risk, my friend. There is nothing more worth that risk."

"I know you care for her, but—"

"The decision is not yours to make, Koda." Shiawase reached out and put a hand on the ghost's shoulder. "And it is not your place to stand in my way."

Koda took a deep breath and closed his eyes. When he opened them again, he looked to Edgar. "What do you need for the ward?"

"There are few things able to channel that much power without disintegrating. One of the most stable looks like a golden Ryō coin. It can host all but the most powerful of wards."

Shiawase frowned. "You will need to be more specific, my friend. The Ryō has a long history, and is perhaps better known as the koban after the Tokugawa

Period."

"I don't know those specifics," Edgar said. "But I know someone who would."

"Ward." Koda glanced between the two. "This is truly the path you wish to walk?"

Shiawase nodded.

"So be it. Seek out Ward. I will visit Adannaya to tell her what's been decided. She should hear this in person so she has someone to yell at."

Edgar smiled. "Better you than me. I'll return to the front. Morrigan is holding the walls on her own, and I have little doubt they could use assistance."

"Be safe, friends," Koda said. "This war is far from done."

CHAPTER TWO

Z OLA GRUMBLED AT the expired sour cream in the fridge at Coldwater. Damian had been the last one there, and it was his turn to restock everything. She turned the tub in her hand and frowned. Would two weeks be that bad? She cracked the lid and sniffed at it. Nothing unusually sharp assaulted her nose.

She shrugged and set the sour cream on the counter. She'd survived worse. Zola reached for the freezer. Now that, Damian had most certainly restocked. She shook her head at the mass of chimichanga packages that had been fit into the small space like a puzzle of frozen bricks.

A pack of ghost pepper chimichangas in hand, Zola turned toward the microwave, only to catch a glimmer of gray from the corner of her eye.

"Zola," the voice said.

In the time it took for her to realize her cane was across the room, her company was nowhere to be seen, and her heartrate had spiked. She summoned a shield, sacrificing her toes as the brick of chimichangas thumped against the ground.

A brilliant blue shield of power stood between her and the interloper. "God*dammit* Koda. Are you trying to kill me before Nudd gets a chance? Shit, boy. Shit." She cursed again and let the shield snap out of existence.

"My apologies, Adannaya."

"Stuff you into a bloodstone with Tessrian is what Ah should do," Zola muttered. She frowned at her foot and wiggled her toes. Satisfied she hadn't managed to break anything, she snatched up the bag of chimichangas and walked through the ghost.

Koda gasped as she passed through him, and she didn't suppress a wicked grin at the ghost's surprise. Necromancers had far more of a presence to the dead than commoners did.

"What brings you?" Zola asked, tossing a chimichanga onto a plate and starting the microwave.

"Our meeting with the council yielded unexpected results."

"How so?"

"Many of the society do not wish to take sides in the conflict."

"Fools," Zola muttered. "What do they think will happen if Nudd takes power? That he'll leave them be?

They hold the knowledge of what he's done. He'll come for them, Koda."

"I know. Vicky seeks the Heart of Quindaro, and Nixie I'm sure will pursue the Eye of Atlantis. Those powers we were already aware of. But there are more."

Zola retrieved her food from the microwave, slopped some sour cream on top, and headed for the front room by the wood stove. She set the plate down and picked up what looked like a piece of a horn.

Koda frowned at it.

"It's the Heart of Quindaro. Fragment of a demon."

"What? Vicky already returned?"

Zola nodded. "She's here with Luna, one of Cama-zotz's death bats. They're out in the woods with the ghosts. Ah admit, Luna's discomfort around ghosts is somewhat amusing. Leave it to Vicky to try to help her 'get over it.' We'll see how well *that* goes."

Koda hesitated, eyeing the Heart of Quindaro before continuing. "Edgar has been speaking to the Society of Flame. Did you know?"

Zola barked out a laugh between bites. "Did Ah know? How in the seven hells would Ah know what's going on in your secret clubhouse?"

"Your alliance with Edgar. I thought he may have told you."

"Ah haven't seen much of Edgar lately. We've both

had our hands a bit full."

"My mistake. You'll understand if concern for secrecy drives many of us in these times."

Zola studied Koda as she stuffed a bite of chimichanga in her mouth that would have made Damian proud. She chewed and swallowed. "Nixie makes for the Eye of Atlantis. That still leaves us short a core to transfer the devil's knot."

"Nixie has gone already? Good, that's good. How did you know?"

"Aideen?" Zola said. No one answered, so she stood up and made her way into the bedroom. "Aideen!"

A bleary-eyed fairy sat up on a small pillow by an oil lamp and blinked. "I'm up. I'm up."

"We have company. Company that surprised me while you were sleeping."

"Quite sure you can take care of yourself." Aideen launched herself up onto Zola's shoulder and yawned. Zola settled onto the couch before Aideen hopped down onto the coffee table and took a seat on a tiny chair carved out to fit the fairy's wings.

"Aideen, greetings," Koda said.

She waved and picked up a thimble filled with cold coffee.

"Go on," Zola said with a wave to Koda.

"Yes, I have new information regarding the cores."

Koda rubbed at the prayer beads around his neck. "A lead on two more of them, and a verdict on anchoring."

Zola leaned toward the ghost as he told them of the Ryō coin, and Shiawase's decision to become the anchor. It didn't surprise her. Happy had been a loyal companion to Vicky since Damian first rescued the ghost. To hear Shiawase was willing to take that risk... it was a risk many of them would have taken in his place. She could only hope Ward would have knowledge of where to find one. They'd likely need his help to draw the binding knots as it was.

"And the other cores?" Aideen asked.

"A tetradrachm, last known to be in the possession of a demon of knowledge. Cursed, or blessed, long ago."

Zola leaned back on the aged green couch. There weren't a great many demons of knowledge. But she knew of one, had spoken to them on more than one occasion, and it looked as though she'd once more be speaking with Ronwe.

"The second," Koda continued, "is a piece of eight stolen from a vampire hoard centuries past. I fear there is less information to help locating the piece of eight."

"Two cores," Aideen said.

"We focus on the one we have a better lead for,"

Zola said.

Koda shook his head. "We don't have a good lead on either of them. Demons are not the most forthcoming of creatures. They require a price too much for mortals to pay."

"Not all of them," Zola said. "Ronwe owes me a favor."

Koda blinked. "How is it a demon owes *you* a favor?"

"A story for another day."

"It sounds as though there's not much we can do until we have the Ryō coin," Aideen said.

Zola opened the wooden trunk beside the coffee table. She pulled out a green stone, shot through with blood red rivers.

"You think Tessrian could help?" Aideen asked.

Zola contemplated it before shaking her head. "Damian's promise to her remains unfulfilled. Ah doubt Tessrian would be willing to share much of anything with his allies." She set the stone back in the trunk.

"There is one other thing," Koda said. "Once you have the cores, you'll need to return to the place the devil's knot was bound in earnest."

Zola cursed. She knew where that was, and she had no desire to visit the heart of the Burning Lands.

"Should you have need, do not hesitate to summon me."

Zola nodded and turned to Aideen. "Wait here for Vicky and Luna. Ah think it's time Ah visit Ronwe."

CHAPTER THREE

B EFORE HEADING OUT, Zola studied the photos of the mosaic beneath Falias for a brief time. The design was troubling her, but she hadn't pinpointed the reason.

She climbed into her '57 Chevy and let the knobs on the back of the steering wheel massage her hands before starting it up. She'd almost gotten lazy about driving, but it felt wasteful to ask Aeros for a ride to Fredericktown.

The gravel road was as bumpy as ever on the way out. Erosion had taken its toll, since loggers had been allowed onto some of the neighboring properties. Folks didn't seem to understand how much those roots and fallen trees affected the flow of water on the hillsides.

She bounced her way over steep hills and narrow curves while the tires crunched on the gravel. Zola took great care to avoid the deeper ruts. It wasn't long before the ruins of long-forgotten homesteads passed by in glimpses through the woods and the dead started to pry at her senses in earnest.

The sawmill town had been gone for centuries now, torn down, collapsed, and decayed to the point a random hiker wouldn't know they stood on the corpse of a bustling mill. But to those who were sensitive to the dead, it was unmistakable. The chill. The crawling feeling of someone watching you in the wilderness. Some days Zola could hear them, the old ghosts, calling out things they couldn't have known in life. But that's something necromancers understood keenly.

The dead were always listening.

Zola left the old aluminum gate open. She'd be back soon enough, and curious locals were the least of her worries. Zola drove past a handful of modern homes as she made her way back to Highway 67. North would take her to Fredericktown. She knew she'd find Ronwe there because she'd helped imprison the demon long ago.

Storm clouds boiled to the west, an eerie sight, as they seemed to move of their own accord, shadowing hills only to split and twist as two fronts collided. Tornadoes weren't uncommon in the area, and that was something Zola had no desire to deal with on the open road. The thought of those violent funnels reminded her of Gurges, and the day they'd lost Cassie. Her knuckles whitened on the wheel. She'd had enough of loss in her many years.

The drive to Fredericktown wasn't long. Twenty minutes once she'd made it onto the highway. Zola passed a curve in the highway that flanked Twelvemile Creek. The creek wasn't visible from the road, but she knew it was there. She and Philip had killed more than one man in its shallow waters. She eyed the treeline, memory pulling her back to an age long since lost.

Zola merged right onto the Highway 67 business loop. A handful of homes and old repair shops lined the road. It wasn't the smallest town she'd spent time in by any means, and small homes grew more dense as she passed the old cemetery on the outskirts.

She drove by several pre-fab buildings before the town square came into view. Red brick and low architecture reminded her somewhat of St. Charles, and a great many Main Streets she'd visited in her life. Some had been far more welcoming than others.

The Civil War museum, an old converted colonial two story, drifted by her window on the left. A short wrought iron fence graced the front lawn, its white paint flaked and fading.

Zola slowed as she reached the library, only a few buildings down from the museum. She sighed and studied the darkened store front. It was clearly closed, and every light in the building was off.

She continued on, circling around the court square, which itself was quite round, leaving the towering brick bell tower of the courthouse behind as she passed a restaurant and a few shops on her way back to the museum.

Ronwe had been bound at the library, but she'd been given more leeway than most. There were a few buildings she could reach, but if the library had closed, Zola suspected she knew exactly where Ronwe would be.

The rumble of the '57 Chevy quieted as Zola pulled up to the curb outside the museum. Zola took a deep breath and took the keys out of the ignition. This wasn't a reunion she was particularly looking forward to. She closed the door with a thump and patted the blue hood of her old Chevy.

A young man walking his small dog down the street stopped. "That's a beautiful car."

Zola offered him a smile. "Thank you. Every bit of the old girl's original."

"She must be worth a fortune."

"Ah suppose, if you parted her out. But that would be a crime."

The man's tiny dog yipped at Zola. She smiled and patted the dog on the head in much the same way she patted her car.

"You ever need work done, I run a little shop on the outskirts of town. I love working on the classics."

Zola smiled. "Ah'll remember that."

"Have a good day, ma'am." He inclined his head and continued on his way.

The city boys could use a lesson from him. Zola straightened her cloak and walked into the museum's front yard, passing the fence that didn't even come up to her knees.

A small black iron bench sat on the left side of the squat porch. A half step of white stone led her up to the front door. Zola couldn't see through the shade pulled over the glass, but when she pushed on the door, it swung open.

Dark hardwood floors waited just inside the foyer. She knew the floors followed through the rest of the house, but she turned to the left and found herself in a room where the walls were covered with old articles and display cases flanked the walls, filled with models, dioramas, and old Civil War artifacts. Zola could still remember using things that looked very much like what now sat in those display cases. But now the bullets had turned white with time, the belt buckles had rotted, and even the steel had started to erode away.

A diminutive woman spun a rack filled with books

and pamphlets. "If you have any questions, don't hesitate to ask. If you're here for the reading, you're a bit early. It's actually not until tomorrow."

She turned toward Zola, the tight bun on her hair crisscrossed with a pair of pencils. In her hand, she held a book on quilting, but she froze when she saw the woman standing behind her.

"Zola Adannaya. What in the seven hells brings you to this old place?"

"Well," Zola said. "It appeared the library was closed, and I figured this was the next best chance I'd find you."

The woman looked down at the book in her hands. "And so you have. Perhaps I've grown somewhat predictable over the years. Or perhaps you and that bastard locked me down in an area where there are only two places I can find books."

Zola offered a cold smile. "You still owe me a favor. We didn't lock you away in a soul stone, and you know damn well we could have. Ah need that favor, Ronwe."

The demon grimaced and made her way to a stool behind the cash register. She opened the book on quilts, and slowly thumbed through the pages, studying the patterns, and absorbing the text far faster than most mortals would be able.

"Phillip's dead."

"That's good to hear. I hope he died bad."

"I killed him. Some days you have to put a rabid dog down."

Ronwe paused and looked up from her book, eyes narrowing. "*You* killed him. That I did not expect. I remember when you were both inseparable. Of course, you also used that time to trap a great many of me and my kin."

"And most will stay imprisoned for eternity."

Ronwe harrumphed. "Eternity. You mortals have no sense of time, or just how long you can stretch it. How long the immortals have lived. How much longer the fairies lived upon the surface of this world than you."

"You have a library. You have a history of this building, and mortals who are interested in discussing it. You have a better life here than you ever would've had in the Burning Lands. You know that. And certainly a better life than being trapped in a soul stone."

"Seventy years," Ronwe said. "Seventy years I lived here, watching this town rise and fall and rebuild itself again. Only then did that library come around."

"I thought time wasn't something we mortals could understand?" Zola said.

Ronwe closed the book and set it on the glass countertop. "What favor do you ask?" She ran her finger along the edge of the cash register. "I do not like living with your sword hanging above my head, Adannaya. Tell me what you seek, and let us be done with it."

"I'm looking for a tetradrachm."

Ronwe tapped a finger on the glass countertop. Her voice rose into the sickeningly sweet tone of a retail clerk who was utterly done with her customer. "Have you tried eBay?"

Zola raised her knobby old cane a few inches into the air and then slammed it down on the hardwood. "Ah'm in no mood, demon. We seek a tetradrachm, one that was last known to be in the possession of a demon. If you have knowledge of it, Ah'd consider our debt paid."

"Last in the possession of a demon?" Ronwe said. "Do you realize how many demons there are in the world? That is as silly a question as asking if I know a random person from Australia."

"Try to remember," Zola said. "This was no ordinary coin. This would have the properties to affect a devil's knot."

Ronwe stopped tapping her fingernail. A slow laugh bubbled up from her diminutive form. It was not the laugh of a human. It was deeper than her voice, holding a promise of darkness and violence most would never suspect. "You already know the demon. One obsessed with wards, who collected the old artifacts like a commoner obsessed with numismatics."

"I don't know what that means," Zola said. "Speak plainly."

"Tessrian," Ronwe said, one side of her mouth inching up just short of a smirk.

"So help me..." Zola started.

"I speak the truth. There is no reason for me not to. I remember what it was like trapped inside that soul stone. To be bound to it in the creation of a blood-stone. I have no desire to return to that prison. My favor to you is done."

"Tessrian is going to be unbearable," Zola muttered.

"Why would that be?" Ronwe asked. "Do you owe favor to the demon?"

"Don't push your luck."

Ronwe laughed. "I shall restrain myself. Speak with Tessrian. If I do not speak the truth, you know where to find me. My prison surrounds the library and comes down to this old house. Not many places to look.

"But I will tell you a secret, Adannaya." When Zola started to protest, Ronwe continued, "At no cost to you. Though I may be unable to leave, and sometimes find my days as a librarian to the mortals trying, the halls of knowledge suit me. The interpretations of men, attempting to perceive the universe around them, are a comedy all their own."

Zola turned away and strode back toward the front door. She cast a glance over her shoulder. "Don't go anywhere."

She would have been lying if she said the irritated look on the demon's face didn't give her some measure of satisfaction.

CHAPTER FOUR

Z OLA'S '57 CHEVY roared as it bounced onto the highway. To say she was irritated with Ronwe didn't quite encompass her current fury. She'd wasted time driving up there, and she was making up more of that time than she should as the car tore down the highway ever faster.

She didn't slow until she reached the turnoff for the gravel road. And even then, she continued faster than she should have, making the shocks work for all they were worth as gravel sprayed the undercarriage. Zola carefully guided the car around the worst of the washout before reaching the field with the cabin.

She drove up the hill and parked close to the old oak. It was far enough away from the walnut trees she wouldn't have to worry about dents. She slammed the door and stalked up the worn wooden steps that led to the front porch.

The screen door squealed in protest, and the spring stretched before it snapped back into place behind her.

The crack of wood on wood as the door closed drew all the eyes in the room to her.

Luna froze with a handful of cheese balls in her mouth. "Vicky said I could have some too."

The wide eyes of the death bat and the obvious concern in her voice caught Zola so off guard, her fury at Ronwe and the time she'd wasted started to bleed away in a whisper of laughter.

Zola walked to the couch and tapped her cane on the floor a few times before settling in.

"Bad news?" Aideen asked.

"Is it ever *good* news, talking to a demon?" Zola muttered. "It wasn't a dead end, but it wasn't the answer Ah wanted to hear, either. Ronwe doesn't know where to find the tetradrachm, but she did tell me who might."

"That doesn't sound all that bad."

Zola's eyes trailed down to the chest on the coffee table. "And she's closer than you could imagine."

"What?" Aideen asked, leaning forward. "You mean Tessrian? Come now, Damian's word to her has gone unfulfilled. She's not going to be willing to help us."

"You going into the bloodstone, Zola?" Vicky asked, stealing a handful of cheese balls from Luna. A small gray furball lurked on the counter behind Vicky,

Jasper's big black eyes studying the room with some interest.

Aideen blinked.

"Damian did it," Vicky said before Aideen could respond.

Zola inclined her head. "Ah am, girl. Ah don't see a way around it."

It was then that the screen door to the front porch squealed. Zola snatched up her cane before she recognized the shadow pushing through doorway. The room fell silent.

"Girl," Zola said, tapping her knobby old cane on the hardwood floor, "Ah've seen three days dead raccoons that looked better than you."

Nixie offered her a small smile from her scarred and ravaged face. "It's been a rough day."

But with the arrival of Nixie and her news, Zola's mood both soured and grew hopeful. The news running on the small television gave Zola confirmation of Nixie's story that she didn't need. Nixie had battled in earnest on the walls of Del Morro in Puerto Rico, and the Unseelie had shown themselves to the commoners.

Nudd had passed the point of what Zola once might have considered a reasonable sanity in a time of war. Now it was clear he'd cracked open gateways for

Abyss creatures all across the world.

At this rate, what didn't die would be corrupted well enough in time. Zola watched somewhat distantly as Vicky crushed Nixie in a hug. Dark times were upon them, and weight she'd not felt in decades settled into her bones. A crushing blackness like utter hopelessness. But she'd been in that kind of darkness before. It was an old friend that only stoked the raging fire it meant to smother.

"Let me take a look at that," Zola said, extending her hand as Nixie rolled the Eye of Atlantis between her fingers.

Aideen went about inspecting Nixie's wounds while Zola studied the Eye. Her concentration didn't waver, other than when she heard Nixie saying something about a poultice that tasted like the bottom of Damian's refrigerator. That … was disturbing.

After a good deal of cursing and healing, Aideen settled back down onto the coffee table.

It didn't take much for Nixie to talk Zola into speaking the incantation over the Book that Bleeds. To harvest whatever weapon waited inside. She knew Vicky worried about the danger to Zola, but this was for Damian. Some risks were always worth taking.

"It's better than letting him die," Vicky said. "I couldn't live with myself if we just let him go."

Zola took a deep breath. "Me either, girl. Me either." She paused and pulled out a small folded sheet of colorful paper. Translucent blood dripped from it for a moment, and then it was gone. "Hold the book upside down? *Aperio tectus vene—*"

"That's the one," Nixie said as she frowned at Zola. "Did Damian write that incantation down on a brochure?"

Zola's lips twitched. "Looks like it, girl." Little more was said as Zola picked up the Book that Bleeds, grimacing at the translucent blood pouring from the damned tome. She turned it upside down and spoke, "*Aperio tectus veneficium!*"

Thunder crashed as a sliver of red hot silver slipped from the binding of the Book that Bleeds, and something else materialized in front of the cabin. A brief panic swept through the cabin before they realized it was Mike the Demon and the little necromancer.

Aideen paced back and forth on Zola's shoulder. "I'm going to be very upset if we blow up."

Mike held his palms out. "I promise no one will explode." And as an afterthought, he added, "Today."

Zola raised the Eye of Atlantis. "What the hell else can we do?" And she spoke the words, "*Omnia Caritas Destuit!*"

The Eye shattered in her hand, tiny fissures racing

around the surface until it collapsed, and a brilliant ball of blue energy remained. It still looked like the Eye of Atlantis, but where before it had been a dull glass, it now had an appearance as if made of fire.

"Two cores," Zola said. "All we need now is the third."

"And an anchor," Nixie said. "Gaia said we'll need an anchor for the devil's knot."

Zola nodded. "Ah know, girl. Ah heard the same from Koda."

"Gaia said …" Nixie trailed off. "Gaia said Damian is fading. We only have a few days, at most."

"Buck up," Zola said. "That just means we have to hurry."

Nixie left to return to the water witches after a short conversation. She'd become their main contact with the commoners, and to sever that tie now could be disastrous. Aideen left for Falias to reunite with Foster and let Morrigan know what was happening.

Zola slipped the Eye of Atlantis into her pocket and looked up at Mike. "Now then, let's you and me discuss our *vacation* to the Burning Lands."

CHAPTER FIVE

"**Y**OU'RE GOING TO step into Tessrian's blood-stone?" Mike asked.

Sarah let out an exasperated sigh and crossed her arms. "That's what she just said."

Mike blinked.

Zola chuckled. "Ah like your attitude."

"I don't think Vicky and Luna are too happy you left them outside," Sarah said.

"Ah think it's best if Vicky stays away from any magic concerning a key of the dead. Now, if Ah get the information we need from Tessrian, we'll have to get to the throne room in the Burning Lands. Hence our vacation."

Mike shook his head. "There's no easy way to the heart of the Burning Lands. Even now, without Prosperine, you'll need to cross the Sea of Souls. And there are a great many inhabitants of the Burning Lands who would rather see you dead."

"See me dead?" Zola said.

"Your apprentice killed their queen," Sarah said. "As far as the demons and the Geryons are concerned, you might as well have killed Prosperine with your own hands."

"Ah suppose we'll worry about that if Ah survive this meeting." Zola ran her finger down the edge of her dagger's sheath. "If Ah don't, Ah leave it to you to negotiate with Tessrian. We need her knowledge to locate the tetradrachm. If Ronwe says Tessrian knows something of it, Ah'm inclined to believe the demon. There's no love between those demons, and if Ronwe can cause Tessrian some misery through us, she wouldn't hesitate."

"I can't step into a bloodstone," Mike said. "My very nature would trap me inside it immediately."

"I wasn't talking to you," Zola said, her eyes flicking up from the dagger in her hand to Sarah.

Sarah clapped her hands together. "I'd be happy to. Not that I want you to die—please don't die—but if you do, you can have faith in me."

Mike cursed under his breath. "We should have just stayed in the Burning Lands."

Sarah frowned at him. "And what if it hadn't been Zola or Nixie unlocking the Eye of Atlantis? That could have been the end of every water witch in existence."

"There was a time that wouldn't have bothered

me," Mike grumbled.

"Yes, well, things change." Sarah reached out and squeezed his arm.

"That they do, girl," Zola said. "That they do. Now, you two stand back."

Mike and Sarah both retreated. They didn't need to be told a second time.

"Last time Damian stepped into a bloodstone, he went with Gaia's aid." Zola unsheathed the key of the dead, running her thumb around the runes and symbols carved into the pommel of the dagger. "Ah'm taking a different path. Ah only hope Damian's notes on the Book that Bleeds are right. Guess Ah won't have to worry for long." She tapped on a small notepad with some of Damian's chicken scratch.

"You better be right about this, boy," she whispered before plunging the key of the dead straight through the bloodstone cradled in her left palm and impaling her hand to the hilt.

She meant to cry out in pain or shock at impact of the blunt blade, but it had cut through her as if it had been the finest scalpel. Then the world turned to blood, fading as rivers of power blinded Zola and silence choked her.

✦   ✦   ✦

CYCLOPEAN PLANES OF crystal intersected like the geometric artistry of a madman. The searing pain of the dagger ebbed, and Zola looked down to find her left hand intact, and the dagger still firmly grasped in her right. Only now the blade was drenched in a rich red.

Footsteps sounded behind her before a grating voice echoed all around. "It is a rare fool who would pay a blood price to open that gateway."

Zola reached up and pulled back the hood of her cloak as she turned toward those footsteps. "A rare fool, indeed."

The shock on the demon's face gave Zola no small measure of satisfaction. Red flesh marred with canyons black as pitch contorted into a snarl. "You dare set foot in this prison? You taunt forces that could destroy you in moments, Adannaya."

"Ah suppose you haven't forgotten our last encounter."

"When you trapped me in this pit?" Tessrian asked, her back straightening and her height increasing until she towered over Zola.

"Ah'm here on behalf of Damian. Here to complete his pact and return you to the Burning Lands."

The looming form hesitated. The rising light in both the demon's hands faded. "How much time has passed since he failed to keep his word?"

Zola gambled, concealing the sly smile that threatened to appear on her lips. "He didn't give you a timeframe. So long as the deed is done before he's done, his word remains unbroken. Your failure to negotiate terms is not his fault."

Tessrian released a hollow laugh and settled onto an outcropping of red crystalline stone. "And what price have you come seeking, necromancer?"

"Only knowledge."

Tessrian's mouth twisted into a cracked line. "Then you should seek out Ronwe. Was it not you who freed her? Or so your apprentice claimed."

Zola closed her eyes for a beat. What in the hell had Damian said to Tessrian? If the boy had been stupid, they were both about to die.

"He didn't lie. He didn't know. Ronwe was freed from her prison, but Ah locked her away in another." Zola looked around at what amounted to a twenty foot cube that was Tessrian's home. "Though her prison is a good deal roomier."

"I sense no lie in your words, Adannaya. I am ... surprised you would release a demon."

"Ah can do the same for you," Zola said, "but better. Ah can return you to the Burning Lands, as Damian promised."

"Then I ask you again," Tessrian said, meeting Zola's gaze with her infinite black eyes. "What is your price?"

"I spoke with Ronwe."

Tessrian leaned back on her seat. But she had no response for that, and showed no surprise. Zola wondered if the demon had already surmised she'd been in contact with Ronwe.

"I seek a tetradrachm. One that was known to be in the possession of demons. Ronwe believes that you may be the only one who knows of it."

Tessrian narrowed her eyes. "And what need would you have for an old coin."

Damian might have gambled the first time he visited Tessrian, and Zola supposed it was her turn to do the same. "We need to re-anchor a devil's knot. The coin would act as a core in the transfer."

"My," Tessrian said. "But you *have* been busy. I suppose if you seek the tetradrachm, you seek the piece of eight."

Zola hesitated. Of any response Tessrian might have given, that wasn't what she expected.

Tessrian lowered herself to the floor, crossing her legs before steepling her fingers. "And the devil's knot… It is bound to your apprentice?"

Zola nodded.

"Then your apprentice is lost."

"That is not for you to decide," Zola said. "But even if it were true, that means Ah'm your last best hope for returning to the Burning Lands. Give me the information Ah seek, and you will sit upon your damned throne."

Tessrian slowly rubbed her fingertips together, her claw-like fingernails scratching at flesh as she stared at Zola. "You necromancers take too many risks with the world. You always have, and it has always been your end. I see no reason not to help you on the journey to your death."

"A favor we shall return," Zola said.

Tessrian smiled. "Then take note of the knowledge Ronwe has kept from you. The tetradrachm and the piece of eight will not aid you in the transfer of the devil's knot. Both are made to bind a Titan, and if you are quite mad, to steal a Titan's power."

"What?" Zola said.

"The very substance of the cores you seek should have told you as much. You befriended the wolf, and fate shows one core will be the Heart of Quindaro. Another the Eye of Atlantis, gifted to you by the water witches, if not taken by force. Powerful magicks in flesh and crystal."

"If that was true," Zola whispered, "where would

we find a third?"

Tessrian crossed her arms and didn't hide the smile on her face. "The bloodstone of Ronwe of course."

Zola's heart sank into her stomach. "That stone was broken."

"Perhaps you can find another, then," Tessrian said, patience bleeding away from her words before she collected herself again.

"Perhaps we can use yours," Zola said, bald malice in her voice.

"And if you destroy me, or free me now to gain access to the bloodstone, what happens if you learn I was lying to you? That's a risk you cannot afford."

Zola wanted to curse, because she knew if that happened everything they were trying to save would be lost, but she didn't give Tessrian the satisfaction. "Tell me where the tetradrachm is."

"Bring me to the Burning Lands. You'll be able to speak with me in the bloodstone without stepping inside. Once I'm there, I'll tell you all you need to know. I will take you to its hiding place, and hand it to you myself."

"Ah accept your terms." Zola slashed the air with the key of the dead until the red wound opened in front of her. She stepped through, leaving the whispers of the demon behind her.

CHAPTER SIX

R ED LIGHT FLASHED all around in sickening bursts before all light left the world. The cabin came back into focus between one breath and the next. Mike, Sarah, Vicky, and Luna all stood at the far edge of the room by the front door.

"Goddamned demons." Zola looked down. The blade glowed white where it had pierced her hand. She pulled in one smooth motion, freeing her hand and the bloodstone at once.

Aideen hopped from the coffee table to the arm of the sofa where Zola collapsed. "Let me see your hand."

Zola held it up, as her brain tried to catch up to her surroundings. The transition had been rough, far rougher than walking into the stone. She'd rather spend a week spiraling through the Warded Ways than step out of the bloodstone again. It had been fast, but the nausea was slow to leave.

"An odd magic," Aideen said, looking up to meet Zola's gaze with a frown. "There is no wound in your hand, and the stone is intact. An illusion?"

Zola held up the key of the dead. "It was no illusion." Blood stained the blade down to its hilt. She studied the blood. She held the blade upright, and the runnels finally stopped, a few closing the distance that kept the hilt from impacting her palm. She leaned forward and let the key of the dead clatter to the tabletop.

"Did you find out where the tetradrachm is?" Vicky asked.

The group slowly filtered back to their seats as Zola shook her head. "It certainly wasn't the answer we were looking for. Tessrian gave us information, but Ah'm afraid we're further from moving the devil's knot than we thought."

"How can that be?" Vicky asked.

"If we choose to believe Tessrian, the tetradrachm and the piece of eight won't act as a core for the devil's knot. They are a different power altogether. And Ah'm sorry to say, her reasoning makes sense."

"Reasoning?" Aideen said. "Reasoning is not what we would normally do with a demon." She glanced at Mike, but the fire demon showed no offense, if he had taken any.

"The Heart of Quindaro and the Eye of Atlantis are both crystals. The tetradrachm is something else.

Perhaps something older, but most assuredly something forged to imprison the Titans. And possibly steal their power."

"But that's good, then," Vicky said. "We may not need them for the devil's knot. We can use them to gift Gaia's powers to Damian."

"Perhaps," Zola said. "If they're for the right Titan. And if Tessrian wasn't lying."

"Unless you or Koda has a better idea," Aideen said. "I think we're still going to need both of them. But what of the devil's knot? What did she tell you about that?"

"The soul stone of Ronwe," Zola growled. "Ronwe knows what I seek. She knows I'm looking to free Damian. She could have guided me onto the right path, and yet here we are."

"I do not trust them," Mike said. "There are too many pieces, too many ways for them to lead you astray, or send you into the jaws of the trap."

Zola let a small smile creep over her lips. "That's why I'm going to get Ronwe's attention."

She slid a piece of parchment from a yellowed envelope in the trunk and picked up the key of the dead once more. Zola wrote a letter in blood as the others watched.

"What are you doing?" Luna asked. "A blood rite?"

Zola glanced up at the death bat. "Of a sort, Ah suppose. It's a letter for a demon."

"You mean to visit a black altar," Mike said. "Adannaya … are you sure?"

She finished the sentence and peered down at the letter.

Betrayal is not forgotten.

Instead of answering Mike with words, Zola lifted a gray candle from a tray inset in the top of the trunk. She struck a match, its eager burn perhaps a sign it had been left on the coffee table for a bit too long. But it lit the candle well enough.

When the wax had pooled, she tilted it onto the folded letter and let it drip. She pulled a bronze seal from the trunk and sank it into the wax, leaving it to set for a moment while she looked up at Mike.

"She lied to me, Mike. A lie of omission, but considering her current imprisonment, Ah'd like to be sure it *never* happens again."

Mike tilted his head. "If you think it best."

"Ah like the old demon, Mike. But she pushes her boundaries. Ah've no desire to break my own word to her. This is the way."

"I'll go with you," Vicky said.

Zola shook her head. "No girl, you stay here with Luna for the time being. Keep the Heart and the Eye safe." She pulled the Eye of Atlantis from her cloak and set it in the trunk along with the Heart of Quindaro. "Hard to find, but not impossible. We gather powers to us, and that will not go unnoticed."

"If you succeed, I suppose that vacation will be in order?" Sarah asked.

Zola gave her a sly grin. "A vacation or a funeral."

"Or both," Luna said. "I've seen some beautiful funerals."

She shook her head. "Ah know you're a death bat, but Ah'm going to do my best to avoid my own funeral for a time."

Luna shrugged and scooped out one more handful of cheese balls from the can on the table.

Mike looked at Sarah. "We should return to the Burning Lands. Time grows short, and I fear the risk outweighs the reward at this moment."

Sarah smiled up at Mike. "That's what I like to hear." She looked to Zola. "We'll camp by the Sea of Souls if we don't die. If *you* don't die, meet us by the forest Damian raised."

"Ah have no idea where that is," Zola said.

"I do," Vicky said. "I can get you there."

Mike looked like he was about to protest, but Sarah's arched eyebrow convinced him otherwise. "So be it."

"We could travel with Gaia and come with you," Vicky said.

"No," Mike said without hesitation. "Do not ever travel close to a black altar through the Abyss. You could be trapped inside a doorway no being remembers, or shatter a gateway between realms."

"Good to know," Vicky said under her breath. "Never mind."

"Be safe." Zola picked her keys up from the coffee table. She eyed the key of the dead before slipping it into her cloak. "There's another can of cheese balls under the sink if you need them."

She patted Sarah's shoulder as she passed. "Keep him out of trouble."

"When have I not?"

Zola smiled to herself as the screen door squealed closed and she made her way back to her car.

CHAPTER SEVEN

I F THERE'D BEEN a decent highway between them, the drive wouldn't have taken that long. The fastest route would be 67 to 34 and south on 49. Better than gravel, which Zola knew was exactly what would be waiting for her closer to her destination.

Mill Spring, Missouri. Unless you lived in the area, it wasn't a place many people knew about. And that wasn't a bad thing. It was the site of an ancient slaughter, demons against men, gods against the dead, and their whispers would haunt the woods until the end of all time.

Zola left the pavement for a gravel road that treated the shocks of the old Chevy with far more gentleness than the road to the cabin.

It was an odd thing how commoners were always drawn to places of old power, though they themselves had no idea what ghost's footsteps they walked in. In the hollows of the old world, long forgotten or never known in the collective consciousness of the commoners, dark things dwelled.

Zola took another right at a four-way intersection of gravel roads. She smiled to herself, amused at just how close the black altar was to the crossroads. A bumpy curve led to a small gravel lot she could park in. Zola turned the car off before slamming the door, breathing in air cleaner than that of even the cabin.

She walked off the lot and made her way through the underbrush until she reached a chain-link fence. The gate opened without protest, more there to keep the unsuspecting from falling into a forty-foot deep pit than to actually restrict entry.

The dead grew into a buzz around her, but it wasn't like the ghosts of the commoners. This was an imprint, a general unease left by the slaughter that once happened there.

Leaves crunched beneath every footfall until Zola stopped on the precipice. Forty feet down waited the bright blue water some referred to as the Gulf. Zola had always known it as the Blue Hole. But regardless of its name, the old collapsed cave held far more history than the commoners knew.

A sharp slope with few handholds led down to the surface of iridescent blue water. Zola's feet slipped on decaying leaves and moss while the scent of mud overtook the world around her. A metallic tang settled

THE BOOK OF THE STAFF

on her tongue, an odd sensation she'd come to recognize when gravemakers were near.

Best to be quick, before it decided to surface.

The story went that the Blue Hole had been a cave that collapsed, a sinkhole fallen into an underground lake. It was an easy lie to believe the way the surface rose and fell with the water table, but to those who knew what to look for, hints of darkness waited all around. And to those who knew how to listen, the forest was never quiet.

Zola sank into the edge of the water, soaking her cloak up to her knees as she settled onto the rocky floor. Before her stood the entrance to the cave. A flooded pit where the undines once battled, and if the stories were to be believed, where an elemental was slain. An Old God, like Aeros, cast down into oblivion.

The altar wasn't buried in the darkness, thank the gods for that. Zola wasn't fond of the old places of the world. Too many ways for magic to go wrong. Too many chances for *things* to find you.

The hair on her arms stood up as a frisson of fear lanced down her back.

Best to be quick.

"*Arcesso altaria.*"

The surface of the water vibrated and flowed to the edges of the lake, splashing against Zola's waist as a narrow altar of black bone rose before her. Charred femurs and bizarre hinged bones from creatures long extinct formed the flat plane of the altar. The skull of a demon, its gnarled horns bonded to bones above, created the pedestal.

Zola let the ley lines flow through her, bending them ever so slightly. She didn't want to accidentally incinerate Ronwe. That would leave them in a world of shit.

"*Infernus Ronwe Accersitus*," she whispered as she drew the letter of blood from her cloak and laid it on the altar. It wasn't unlike the ritual Damian had once used to commune with Azzazoth, but the call to Ronwe would be a great deal less subtle.

The scarred altar burst into flames and rolling, swiveling bones swallowed the letter. But instead of merely relaying a message, the very air began to shake around Zola. Droplets of water popped from the surface of whitecaps as the lake vibrated with malice.

It was only a shadow at first. Wisps of rising steam that absorbed the light. Then the edge of the altar bent as the hand formed, and the air spun, picking up water and debris and flinging it all around until the shadow took shape.

Pungent brimstone tainted the air, and then Zola wasn't the only one breathing in the depths of the Gulf.

"Betrayal?" Ronwe said through gritted teeth. The demon closed her eyes and slowly peeled her hands away from the altar. "Do you have any idea how much that burns? To be pulled through a summoning circle? Torn through the runes of the prison that you chained me to?"

Zola smiled at the demon. "This is not a time for games, Ronwe. Ah wanted to make that *explicitly* clear for you. Do we understand each other now?"

"There are more civil ways," Ronwe said.

"You lied to me."

Ronwe grimaced. "Omitting the facts is not the same as lying."

Zola let out an exasperated breath. "Why didn't you tell me about the bloodstone?"

"It is not as if a broken bloodstone is the only arti-fact of power that may suit your needs. And it was my prison, Adannaya. You should understand that better than most. I never want to see that thing again, and if its magicks were used against me once, I need not tell you the rest."

"Ah could have killed you a hundred times over by now. And Ah've never harmed you. Ah know what you've done in that community, for that community. Ah want to trust you and yet Ah can't."

Ronwe's voice was quiet, the water had stilled

around their feet. "It could kill you all. You don't understand what you seek."

"Then for fuck's sake, tell me."

Ronwe sighed. "The bloodstone was bonded to an Old God, to enhance their power even as it spared their life. For the Titan, you will need the blessing of a priestess, a green witch. I tell you in good faith, the magic must be anchored to the earth itself if you hope to survive."

Zola frowned at the demon.

"The fragments of the bloodstone were buried at Corydon. I'm sure you recall, yes?"

"How could Ah forget? It was stolen from our cache at Gettysburg before it turned up at Corydon. Unleashed by some idiot Confederates. That was a battle that didn't need to happen."

"Perhaps," Ronwe said. "But it was not the Confederates who set me free."

"No one else was there," Zola said.

"Oh, child," Ronwe said. "Philip Pinkerton released me from that stone. I carried my own prison to Corydon."

"No," Zola said, her eyes widening.

"It's distasteful what was done there, but a bargain is a bargain. And I keep my word, Adannaya. I always have. I cleansed my palette in the blood of the second battle of Fort Wagner, as the commoners named it."

"Philip…" Zola squeezed her eyes shut. "Ah was so blind to what he was."

"If you seek out the remnants of that bloodstone, know my prison will not be so easy a target. You know what waits beneath the mooring post."

Zola's voice hardened. "Then it's time to set an old wrong right."

"Heed my words, Adannaya. The guardian there is beyond you. Do not face him alone." Ronwe looked into the black water at her feet. "Of course, that is only if you get out of here alive. You violated the altar by pulling me through, Zola. You never should have summoned me here. This is not my doing."

As Ronwe's form faded, unbidden by Zola, the screams came calling.

CHAPTER EIGHT

Z OLA'S SCREAM JOINED the cacophony when the blue water turned black, and a grip like steel threatened to crush every bone in her ankle.

Dead, milk-white eyes opened in the water, rising to the surface as Zola struggled to free herself. She blasted the thing with a fire incantation so fierce the superheated water scorched her own flesh as it faded. Ice did nothing. Air was useless.

Instinct took over. She had to slow it down long enough to escape, to climb out, but gods only knew what would happen. The only blade on her came into her hand, and she plunged the key of the dead into the heart of the gravemaker.

Whispers rose around her.

Only a moment. Zola, I can only hold it for a moment. Run!

Tears cut through the panic in Zola's chest as she recognized the voice. But it wasn't possible. Damian was trapped in the Abyss, lost to them, lost to himself.

Run, goddammit!

With one violent twist, Zola tore the key of the dead from the gravemaker's chest. She lunged, her ankle pulling free so slowly she thought time itself might have frozen. But then the water splashed around her as she used the dagger for leverage on the steep slope out of the Gulf.

A glance back showed her that black water and the hollow eyes of the gravemaker staring up at her.

"You're losing your damned mind, woman. Pull your shit together."

Her breaths came fast and shallow, but it didn't slow her sprint through the woods. Small branches and twigs snapped off as they snagged her cloak, as twisted as the gravemaker who had come to claim her. She raced back to the car, where she slammed the door and crushed the accelerator. Gravel pinged and sprayed into the woods as Zola sped away from that damned place.

✦   ✦   ✦

THE POUNDING OF Zola's heart slowed as she reached pavement once more. On a straighter stretch of road, she grabbed her phone and said, "Call Ashley cell." The line rang through after a time.

"Hello?" a groggy voice said.

"Ashley," Zola said. "You just getting up, girl?"

"Hey, I got stabbed. I'm allowed to be lazy for a couple days."

"Not today. We're going to need your blessing. The magic of the devil's knot has to be anchored to the earth, or this transfer could kill all three of them."

"The blessing of who?" Ashley asked.

"The blessing of a green witch. A priestess."

The line was quiet for a time. "I'm not a green witch anymore, Zola."

"The hell you aren't. That coven still follows you, girl. That makes you more priestess than anyone else I know."

"I'm not worthy, Zola. I can't put everyone at risk."

Zola mashed the accelerator and her car roared as she passed a slow-moving truck. "Put them at risk? That's been a group effort, girl. Not doing this is putting them at risk."

"I can't lose them. I can't lose them like that, Zola."

Before Zola could respond, the line went dead.

"God damn it," she muttered to herself. "Damn kids and their identity crises. Damian worried about becoming a dark necromancer. Ashley worried she's no longer a priestess of the green witches. Sam worried about being the weak link between Damian and Vicky. Ah've had quite enough."

Zola called another number.

"This is Beth."

"Elizabeth?" Zola said.

There was a sigh on the other end of the line. "Ashley is really the only one I let get away with calling me Elizabeth. And that damn werewolf."

Zola would have laughed if she wasn't gritting her teeth. Hugh had a way of calling you whatever the hell he wanted to call you. "We're going to need Ashley for a ritual. And it's one only a green witch can perform."

"That shouldn't be a problem," Beth said. "So why are you calling me?"

"Because for some reason, that fool doesn't think she's worthy. Ah need you to talk some sense into her. We need her for this, Beth. Ah don't trust anyone else to offer their blessing for the devil's knot."

"Dammit," Beth said. "The more she's embraced the blade of the stone, the more times I've heard her say that. But it's not how I feel. It's not how the coven feels. We'll do what we can. But Zola…"

"Yes?" Zola said after a beat.

"I can't make you promises about this. She's walking a different path than all of us now. You know that."

"We're all walking a different path. Every last one of us. Do what you can. If it goes wrong, perhaps it's time for someone else in the coven to become the priestess."

Beth hesitated at that. It struck a chord, as Zola knew it would. She didn't like manipulating her friends. But occasionally desperate times called for being a bitch.

"I'll be in touch." With that, Beth disconnected.

Zola patted the steering wheel. "Now we're in some shit, aren't we, girl? Yes, we are." She pushed the accelerator down harder, and the car roared its agreement.

✦   ✦   ✦

ZOLA PARKED OUTSIDE the cabin and hurried up the stairs. She paused at the front door, staring at the railing that was so much newer than the rest of the porch. It stood out like a billboard. She remembered Damian flying through that railing when she taught him to use a demon's aura against itself. One lesson of any hundreds she'd taught him in that place.

She flexed her jaw and stormed inside.

"Did you get what you needed?" Vicky asked, shrugging into her backpack.

Zola eyed her and Luna. "Where do you two think you're going?"

"Wherever you are," they answered in unison.

Vicky grinned at Luna before turning back to Zola. "Well?"

"Ah got what we needed." She gave a sharp nod. "And more that we didn't." She pulled the key of the dead out of her pocket and set it back in the trunk. "We're going to Corydon."

"What's a Corydon?" Luna asked.

"A small town in Indiana," Zola said. "More importantly, a battlefield where Ronwe's bloodstone is hidden."

"Let's go!" Vicky pulled her backpack off one shoulder and rooted through it for a moment until she pulled out the dead gray flesh of the hand of Gaia. "I've got jerky and a couple waters too, if you need a snack."

"You have ammunition?"

Vicky lit a soulsword. "I've always got that."

"For the pepperbox. You may need to keep your distance in this fight." She looked to Luna. "Both of you. This place has a guardian. Not unlike Aeros."

"Aeros can be pretty slow," Luna said. "That shouldn't be a problem."

Zola grimaced. "Fulvus is different. A shapeshifter of sorts. Best case is we distract him while one of us retrieves the bloodstone."

Vicky nodded. "Sounds easy enough."

"That's what makes me worry," Zola said, tightening the rope belt around her waist. "Ready?"

Vicky shrugged into her backpack again and held out her hand. Zola and Luna both grabbed hold while Vicky laced her fingers into the hand of Gaia. The world vanished into darkness.

CHAPTER NINE

"**Y**OU BRING COMPANY," Gaia's ethereal voice said before the golden motes of her body had coalesced.

"Hi Gaia," Vicky said.

Zola felt the girl squeeze her hand. It made her smile, the thought that a child, a teenager now no less, showed that kind of small compassion. The golden path illuminated beneath their feet, stretching to the distant stars of the Abyss.

"It is good to see you all here. There was a brief moment where I feared Damian had been lost, but the colossus was brought under control once more."

"When?" Zola asked.

Gaia looked upon her, golden eyes narrowing as she studied her. "A short time ago. But the magic I sensed on him stains you as well."

"Gods, it was him," Zola whispered.

"What?" Vicky asked.

"At the altar. A gravemaker had me. Ah stabbed it

with the key of the dead. It was just a reflex."

Gaia turned to the horizon. "There is not much magic stronger than that for a necromancer. The keys are few, but their power has not eroded over time. Damian's inundation with the gravemakers may have consequences reaching further than I realized."

"He's still in there." Zola's voice cracked, but not even the rising anger in her chest could burn away the tears gathering at the corners of her eyes.

"For now." Gaia's musical voice was a contrast to the dire warning her words delivered. "Where do we journey today, young one?"

"Corydon," Vicky said. "It's a battlefield in Indiana."

"Would you like to see Damian before you depart?" Gaia asked.

Vicky looked to Zola.

"No," Zola said. "We're short on time as it is." What she didn't say aloud was that she didn't need to see him trapped inside that thing. Ronwe's words about Philip had pierced her heart, and she had no desire to be crushed by her emotions.

Luna held on to Vicky's arm a little tighter, looking up at the Titan with plain apprehension.

"We have arrived. Release my hand, and I shall return to Damian."

"Thank you," Vicky said. "We'll be back."

"I hope that is so, little one."

The stars spun like Zola had been punched in the temple, only to switch to a tremendous falling sensation, and then nothing as they stumbled out of darkness and into the light before a log cabin.

✦   ✦   ✦

THE CABIN WAS new, and certainly hadn't been there the last time Zola had set foot on the battlefield. But as she looked around, and took in the small parking lot and paved drive leading away from the area, she realized there were a great deal of things that hadn't been there.

A cannon sat beside them on carefully laid bricks beneath the drooping branches of a gnarled tree. Two tourists wandered about the cabin, which explained why Luna had suddenly launched herself to the rooftop out of sight.

Commoners might be aware they weren't alone in the world now, but seeing a death bat could still cause a scene. And that they didn't need.

While they waited for them to leave, Zola wandered to a ruined stone structure. She didn't remember what it used to be, but it had been destroyed a long time ago, judging by the even decay of the mortar and stone.

She followed an asphalt walking path while Vicky bent over to read one of the monuments. Zola saw it as she turned, behind a low split-rail wooden fence. A simple black post she knew had a massive chain attached to it. The sight alone felt like a weight in her gut.

Zola made her way over to it, the octagonal sides with seven small holes surrounding one large in the center. One bolt was all that held the chain together now. One seal to lock the beast away.

She looked up when an engine started, catching sight of the tourists leaving the area. It was time. Zola waved to Luna when the snow-white head peeked around the side of the cabin. Luna grabbed Vicky on her way, and soon enough they were standing beside Zola.

"That's it?" Vicky asked. "I thought it would be bigger."

"It's a few feet high with plates nearly as big as your head, girl. How big do you think a mooring post needs to be?"

"I might have a better guess if I knew what a mooring post was," Luna said.

"You anchor a ship to it."

"Then what's an anchor for?"

Zola blinked at the death bat. "Let's not worry about that for now. Let's worry about the thing we're about to wake up. Intentionally wake up, at that, gods help us."

She didn't say it out loud, but the thought that Philip had betrayed her here too crawled through her mind. So much damage that man had done to the world. He'd wanted to change things, but damn if she'd ever seen someone go about it in worse ways.

Zola tapped away at her phone briefly.

Last core at Corydon. If we fail, find the Old God.

She slid the phone back into her cloak, only to find Vicky had been watching her text.

Vicky shook her head. "If we fail, we'll be dead."

"No girl. If we fail, you run like hell from this place. Go back through the Abyss and come back in force." Zola grimaced. "This is my mess, girl. And I intend to make it right."

Vicky didn't press her again, but Zola doubted the girl had any intention of running, no matter what happened.

"So this thing is under the post?" Luna asked.

Zola leaned toward the mooring post and laid a hand on it. "If you dug beneath us, you'd only find iron and mud. Once the bond is broken, the Old God will awaken. Keep your distance. He's more molten metal than stone."

"We're fighting a volcano?" Luna said.

"Ah wish that description was less accurate. Now back the hell up." Zola moved her hand to the bolt holding the anchoring chain down. "Fulvus, god of metals. Ah've come back with your fate."

With one swift twist of her wrist and a spark of crystalline ice, the bolt shattered in Zola's hand.

CHAPTER TEN

ARTH AND MUD and stone erupted like a crate of
dynamite had been set off. A wave of heat rolled
off the nine-foot-tall mass as water and mud sizzled on
the creature's skin. Fists and the sleek bronze of the
Old God's flesh grew clear as he stretched, releasing a
roar to shake the earth around them.

Where Aeros was bulky and stone, Fulvus was
made of smooth planes of metal that slid silently over
each other. But as they separated, or the beast flexed,
Zola caught glimpses of stone and the molten core
within. One might mistake Fulvus for an abstract
collection of polygons until the steam forced the
remaining debris away from the god's face.

She'd seen Fulvus once before, when he'd escaped
his original imprisonment and they'd had to bind him
once more, decades later. She hadn't realized why his
eyes looked so different then, like shattered orbs, too
small for that angular face of bronze.

"Oh fuck, that's creepy," Vicky said.

Zola growled in agreement. "We only need his eyes. The rest is fair game. Take him!"

Fulvus didn't speak. He moved. Diamond-like structures of aged bronze shifted forward as if they were armor upon his legs. The Old God splayed his fingers and jets of molten metal burst forth toward Zola.

"Old tricks," Zola muttered. "*Impadda!*"

An electric blue shield sprang to life, sizzling as the metal crashed against it, only to solidify as it fell to the earth. Fulvus changed the angle of his attack, and Zola cursed when the molten metal hit the top of her shield and bounced over it.

Tiny drops of superheated iron and bronze scorched her cloak, and she shouted as some of the metal found her skin. Another shield formed above her as Vicky slid in behind Zola, creating a shell nothing would get through.

Fulvus roared, and between one beat and the next, the god glowed with fire, his fist smashing into Zola's shield hard enough to slide her back. Another blow, and a tiny webwork of cracks etched their way out from the electric blue center.

The Old God pulled back again, only this time Zola dropped her shield and slammed her staff into the earth.

"Orbis Tego!"

A circle shield exploded into life around them, crashing against the Old God's waist and arm and sending him to the ground.

Zola caught a glimpse of white from the corner of her eye. "Stay back!"

"I do not take commands," Fulvus said, rising to one knee before stretching to his full height. "Zola Adannaya."

So he hadn't realized it was Luna she was talking to. Good. The last thing she needed at that moment was a way for Fulvus to leverage them out of the circle shield.

Time imprisoned had not taken a toll on the Old God.

"You free me only to imprison me once more?" The craggy bronze mouth lifted into a mockery of a smile. Above it, the glowing crystalline eyes of the shattered bloodstone. The molten flesh within gave the stone an eerie red glow, stained with green. "You are a strange people."

Vicky let her shield fall, its golden light tracing spirals and jagged runes through the air before flickering out. "What the hell is he talking about?"

"It doesn't matter now, girl." Zola whispered. "Ah'll tell you all about it when we aren't dead."

"This will be your last opportunity for that," Fulvus

said. "But tell me, why have you released me? Your logic appears as flawed as the bearded one's."

Even though Fulvus hadn't named Philip, it was like a punch in the heart. It didn't matter the distance she had, how many wrongs he'd committed, there was always some small part of her that remembered the man he could have been. And perhaps, for a brief time, the man he was.

Did Fulvus understand how much time had passed since those days? Did the Old Gods sense time the same way the rest of the world did? Or was this simply Fulvus waking up and assuming the same things were still happening.

His eyes flared brighter in the shade of the forest. "Why awaken me now?"

"Ah need your eyes," Zola hissed, and the words held enough promise to make the Old God stand up straighter.

Fulvus held out his left arm, and Zola watched as the planes of his skin split and molten metal poured forth. White-hot legs rose before a paunchy torso took shape, and a bearded head.

In moments, Zola was staring into a simulacrum's face, one that wore Philip's likeness. The metal cooled, and the resemblance faded somewhat as crystalline planes of metal obscured the golem's appearance.

"You bastard," Zola whispered.

Fulvus gestured with his right arm, and a shower of molten metal formed the body of another golem. This one was smaller, younger, and as the face of the child Zola had once cared for took shape, rage washed over her. She knew those tight curls, those doe eyes, and she knew the werewolf he'd become.

"When Ah tell you to run, girl, you get Luna and get the fuck away from here."

"I'm not leaving you, Zola."

Vicky flinched when the old necromancer looked at her.

"This is *my* fight. Now *run!*"

The instant the shield fell, Vicky darted into the forest line.

"Emotional creatures, aren't you?" Fulvus said. "Kill them."

The two golems started forward. Zola dropped her cane and held her arms out in front of her, index fingers and thumbs forming a triangle, a focus. She closed her eyes and whispered to herself as heat washed against her face.

Zola's eyes snapped open and she felt the snarl on her lips as the words tumbled from her mouth. "*Magnus Glaciatto!*"

The shift from the heat of molten metal to deepest

cold of the Abyss splintered grass and earth and the mud around their feet. Zola's incantation rose into a scream as her eyes flashed wide and she channeled more line energy than she'd ever dared.

A frigid vortex of ice and power tore through her focus, stealing the warmth from her fingers, blistering her flesh with cold. Frozen daggers of crystal and death punctured the golems, sending sprays of molten blood to splash back onto Fulvus, who himself reeled in the storm.

Memories returned unbidden. Times when she'd been forced to murder people for the mere chance they might endanger her family, the children they'd taken under their wing. And it was times like those, in the darkest moments, when she had sometimes understood the misguided actions of Philip Pinkerton. Had the Confederates caught them in Corydon, they would have been slaughtered. At best, hung. But more likely tortured, raped, or a litany of both.

And now ... and now this thing, this Old God, this mistake, stood between her and Damian. One of the last children she'd sworn to protect. One of the last people she'd promised to never fail.

She broke contact with the focus and aimed her powers to the skies above.

The golems were crawling toward her now, frost set

upon their fiery flesh. But above them, the daggers grew into swords, and Zola bade them fall.

"You cannot match—"

The words of the Old God were cut off by a shower of icy blades, pinning the golems to the earth and impaling Fulvus's head. The Old God staggered, and then roared. He flexed, bronze skin shattering along his right arm as he flung it at Zola. Metal solidified in air, and Zola cried out when the javelin pierced her stomach and embedded itself in the tree behind her, pinning her down.

"That is *enough!*" the Old God roared as he raised his arm.

Zola moved to raise a shield, but her arm wasn't working right. "*Impadda!*" The shield flickered to life for a brief moment, just enough to deflect another projectile, but the impact slammed her arm against the spike in her gut.

"Fuck," she spat, the taste of blood metallic on her tongue.

Fulvus raised his arm again. "Goodbye, Sarah."

Zola grinned at the Old God with bloodied teeth. The name she'd carried when he first met her, Sarah. The name Alan had known her by. The name Philip had whispered when they weren't alone.

The strike came fast, but Luna was faster, striking

from the sky with her arms outstretched. The razor-like edge of her wing sliced through the Old God's shoulder, and they roared together. Fulvus's arm collapsed, still holding the spear of white-hot metal.

But Luna screeched. A cloud of smoke rose up from the death bat's wing as she crashed to the earth, spiraling across it, kicking up mud and grass until she came to a rest on the pavement. Blistered flesh and scorched fur ran from her shoulder to the bottom of her wing where it hadn't been burned away.

Gunshots rang out, shattering the head of the golem who'd had Philip's face.

"Run!" Zola cried out, despair clawing at her chest as she watched the child close on the Old God.

Vicky pulled the second trigger. Fulvus's jaw cracked and bled molten metal as the Old God screamed. She lunged with a soulsword a moment later, but the Old God was too fast. He spun to the side, leaving shattered fragments of his legs behind. An iron backhand sent Vicky to the ground.

Fulvus rose to his feet above her, looking from Zola to the two he'd beaten into the earth. "Passion will always get you killed, mortals."

He raised his arm to strike the final blow against Vicky.

Zola raised a shaky right hand. "*Magnus Glac-*

ciato!" The world was nothing but pain as the unfocused line energy ripped across the field, piercing Fulvus once more, and drawing his attention back to the old necromancer.

Time. Time was all she could give them now. Her shout stretched out as she pleaded with Vicky and Luna. *"Run!"*

"You offered more of a battle than I expected, Zola Adannaya. Die satisfied, knowing that."

Zola spat blood onto the Old God's feet where it sizzled. "Ah won't be the last who comes for you."

The air distended between them. Zola didn't know what magic Fulvus was about to summon, but it was like nothing she'd seen before. A pit as black as any part of the Abyss she'd ever seen stretched out before her, the edges fringed in gray.

A scream rose, and she wondered if it was her own before the winged ball of fire erupted from the blackness. It spun Fulvus around, flames rising from the newcomer's eyes, but the sharp lines of his face were familiar.

His scream was not human.

Fulvus was pulled up into the air in a hurricane of fire that swelled to encase the black and white wings, patterned like an Atlas moth.

"Foster …" Zola whispered.

The spiraling mass rocketed down into the log cabin, sending the entire clearing up in a fireball. Vicky was on her feet now, dragging Luna closer to Zola.

Roars and screams and curses rose up from the chaos of the ruined cabin. A tall shadow stumbled backward, flames streaming from the stump of Fulvus's shoulder.

"You bathe me in the fires I was born from, fool!" Fulvus cried out in laughter and pain.

Foster raised a flaming sword, blue fire spiraling up from the hilt as he closed on Fulvus.

The Old God hurled a javelin of metal at the fairy, but it melted away in the torrent of power around Foster.

Foster growled. "You think you'll leave here alive?"

Whatever Fulvus had been about to say was lost to the ringing impact of the flaming sword plunging through his face.

CHAPTER ELEVEN

"**W**HAT THE FUCK were you thinking, Zola?" Foster shouted as he closed on them.

"My fight," Zola grumbled. "Get the eyes. Ronwe's bloodstone."

Foster reached out to the spike of metal pinning her to the tree.

"Ah said get the damn eyes," Zola snapped. "That's why we're here."

Foster paused and cocked his head to the side. "Nothing else matters?" He gestured to the inferno that had been the cabin. Vicky and Luna huddled to the side of the asphalt leaning up against the fence. "Nothing?"

Zola leaned back against the tree and grimaced. "Get the damned eyes."

"I'll get the damned eyes as soon as you aren't dying on this fucking tree."

Zola made to snap back at Foster again, but a seizure of pain silenced her. "Get it over with, then."

"On three."

Zola nodded as Foster placed his hand on the javelin of metal. But before he even said "one," he ripped the entire length out of her abdomen. As she fell, the motion sent waves of pain through her body like an electric fire.

Foster began his work.

"*Socius sanation,*" the fairy whispered, and the world dimmed as a light without illumination glowed around Foster's hands. He moved her again, and this time the world shifted to darkness.

✦   ✦   ✦

ZOLA AWOKE TO the sounds of whispers, whispers that grew as her senses returned. Vicky was sitting next to her, while Foster worked on Luna.

"It looks pretty good," Foster said.

"Feels better," Luna said, flexing the pale pink flesh that had been scoured of white fur.

Foster turned to Zola when she sat up, the leaves crunching beneath her legs. "You're awake. I suppose I shouldn't be surprised. You've always been resilient."

Zola prodded at her abdomen. The pain was there, but the fact it was only a dull ache made her wonder how long she'd been unconscious.

"What would you have done?" Foster asked. "What

would you have done if I hadn't come? If Morrigan hadn't been there to send me through one of her portals?

She stretched her back and gave Foster a flat look. "Died, I suspect."

Whatever answer Foster had been expecting, that wasn't it. He paused and eyed Zola for a time. "No time to get ourselves killed. You put Vicky and Luna at risk. Why?"

"To save them. That's the final core at your feet. With that, we can move the devil's knot."

Foster picked up the lifeless bronze head of Fulvus, the distended jaw bent at a terribly unnatural angle. "We're spread too thin, Zola. We can't afford more losses. The leviathans are at our gates, and reports of the Eldritch creatures have been heard more than once."

"Nixie fought one at Del Morro," Zola said.

"Nudd's balls," Foster spat.

"But we know more now," Zola said. "Once we move the devil's knot, we know where to begin to claim the cores to grant Damian Gaia's powers. He spoke to me, Foster. When I used the key of the dead, Damian spoke to me. He's not gone yet."

The fairy closed his eyes and his wings sagged. He took two deep breaths and unsheathed the dagger at his belt. With one swift strike, he lodged it beneath the bloodstone in the metal face of the Old God. One more strike, and the first half came loose.

Foster let the jagged edges of the bloodstone roll around in his palm. He closed it in his fist and took a deep breath. "Be more careful next time. And be thankful there will be a next time."

Zola looked away for a brief moment. "We can't let anything stop us, Foster. Nothing."

The fairy ran his fingers through his hair, but he said no more.

"You know we don't have much time, right?" Vicky said. "Gaia said Damian is fading. If we don't take risks, we're all going to die."

Foster jammed his dagger behind the other eye and popped it out of the Old God's face. "I know. Nixie sent word. Honestly if she hadn't, I might not have come here. And you three might be dead."

"Camazotz would've taken care of the rest," Luna said. "Once he's rested, he could bring Nudd down."

Foster offered Luna a smile. "I don't doubt that he could. But can he take on all the eldritch to get to him? The Unseelie Fae? That I don't know."

"Can *we*?" Luna asked.

Foster met Zola's gaze. Neither of them answered Luna's question. They'd both seen enough battles to know what was coming. Death might be the domain of the necromancers, but war could surpass their worst expectations.

"We still need Ward," Zola said. "He made the devil's knot. Ah doubt we know anyone more likely to be able to draw the wards and knots we may need."

"And how do we go about tracking him down? He's been a ghost since he left with the Old Man."

"Happy is looking for them in Gorias." Zola glanced at Vicky. "He wants this to work as much as any of us. Maybe more."

"Faerie is a dark place these days," Foster said. "It's dangerous for anyone there."

"Then perhaps a ghost was the best chance we have to slip through."

Foster frowned and then nodded. "It might be, Zola. It just might be. Let's get you home."

Zola muttered at Foster, an edge of defiance to her voice. "If you think Ah'm letting you drag me through the Warded Ways in this kind of shape, you're out of your damned mind."

Foster turned Zola's hand over and dropped the fragments of Ronwe's bloodstone into her palm. "Walk with Gaia, then. Take care of yourself."

"Ah want to show you something before you go." Zola reached into her cloak and pulled out her phone.

"Damian took these photos of the mosaic beneath Falias." She flipped through a few images before turning it to Foster. "What do you see?"

Foster took the phone and frowned. "The work of a madman."

"Look closer, Foster."

The fairy studied the image, zooming in and squinting at different areas. "Most of the scenes are from the Mad King's reign."

"But how are they arranged?"

Foster cocked his head to the side. "No way." He traced the outline winding between one scene of violence to the next, and his eyes shot up to Zola. "That's impossible. At the center of each spiral of tiles there's a stone."

"A crystal," Zola said. "And the lines connecting them all form the pattern of a devil's knot. Timewalker magic."

Foster shook his head. "Fairies aren't timewalkers. They never have been. What use would they have if they're practically immortal to begin with?"

"Ah'm not concerned with that," Zola said. "This has been bugging me since I noticed it. Look at the edge, here." She pointed to wisps of blue tiles leading away from the devil's knot pattern. "What does *that* lead to?"

Foster shrugged. "I don't know, but do you really think this is the time to worry about a mosaic that's over a thousand years old?"

"Ah've seen what the Fae mosaics can do, Foster. Ah've seen the carvings on the gates of Falias change. Who's to say that didn't happen here?"

"I don't think so. Look, all the scenes here are still images of the Mad King's reign. Nothing's changed."

"What if it was in the process? Why wouldn't that fairy have completed his work if he'd been trapped down there for a thousand years?"

"We can look into it if we live."

Zola grabbed Foster's wrist in an iron grip. "Listen to me. We thought we needed to set the cores into an exact replica of a devil's knot, but what if that's *wrong*. What if that trail, that line, shows us the pattern we need."

"If there was a different pattern, it would have been in the Book that Bleeds."

"We can't *read* the book, Foster. Not all of it."

That gave the fairy pause. "We need to ask Ward. He drew the original devil's knot. Maybe he'll know better how to move it."

"Ah agree."

"I need a print of those photos," Foster said.

Zola pulled up a map on her phone. "Library's only

a mile from here. Let's go." She grunted as she climbed back up to her feet, cringing at the echo of the burn in her gut. Zola took a deep breath and started toward the road.

"We're going to walk a mile?" Foster asked. "In the daylight? To a library? With a death bat?"

"Ah'm sure the librarian has seen stranger things than us."

Sirens roared in the background as the log cabin continued smoldering.

"Time to go."

CHAPTER TWELVE

"**I**'M SORRY, MA'AM," the librarian said, staring at Luna while she spoke to Zola. "We don't have that sort of printer here."

Zola looked around the beautifully decorated and quite modern library. "Ah'm surprised to hear that." When she turned back to the counter, the woman was looking down at Zola's blood-soaked clothes, and the scorched holes from her fight with Fulvus.

"Do you need me to call the police? Are you in danger?"

A slow smile made its way across Zola's face. "Don't worry, girl. Ah can handle myself."

The librarian blinked.

"Oh, enough of this," Foster grumbled, climbing out of Zola's hood and hopping down onto the counter. "Yes, some of us are fairies, no we're not dying, but we really need a printer."

"I ... I suppose you could email it to me?"

"See!" Foster said, turning back around to Zola. "If

you just tell them the situation, they're more than willing to help out."

Zola raised an eyebrow as the librarian started rolling up a magazine into a very tight cylinder. Zola shook her head rapidly.

"What?" Foster asked as he turned back to the woman.

She made a sound that was somewhere between a meep and a squeak.

Foster eyed the magazine and let out an exasperated sigh. "For fuck's sake, lady."

"Language!" the librarian hissed in a quiet but stern voice.

"Is this better?" Foster asked, hopping off the desk and exploding into his full height.

"Glitter!" a little girl squealed behind them.

"Rage glitter," Vicky muttered, looking over the family of three who were ogling the death bat and the fairy in their library.

The librarian looked down at the rolled up magazine in her hand and then back to Foster. She set the cylinder of paper down and gently flattened it out once more. "Yes, well, we have some large mosquitoes around here. I apologize for mistaking you for one."

Foster narrowed his eyes. "You apologize for mistaking me for a *mosquito?*"

"Yes, yes I do." The librarian picked up a pencil, fumbling it for a moment before she scribbled something down and turned it toward Foster and Zola. "Send it to this email address. I'll get it printed out for you."

"I'm happy to pay extra for the annoyance," Zola said. She eyed Foster. "It's easy to mistake him for a mosquito."

Vicky snorted a laugh as Foster gave Zola a surprised, yet slightly annoyed, yet greatly amused look. Zola selected the photos she needed printed and emailed them to the librarian. It took a short time for them to send, but the librarian's computer dinged a moment later.

The librarian's fingers blurred across her keyboard, and two quick clicks of the mouse brought the printer to life behind her. She looked up at Zola. "No charge. If anyone should be apologizing for the inconvenience it should be me. Your…" She eyed the party as a whole. "Your appearance caught me by surprise, and I apologize for that. I'm sure we'll be seeing more of you in the coming years, and we need to get used to it. I don't know, I guess I just thought somewhere as off the beaten path as Corydon would be isolated longer. I'm sorry. I'm rambling."

"You're taking this really well," Luna said. "I don't

know what everyone else thinks, but I don't think you have anything to apologize for. We look a little weird."

"I thought you were wearing a mask at first," the librarian said, pulling the photos off the printer.

Luna's ears twitched. "That usually works out okay on Halloween."

"Camazotz lets you out for Halloween?" Vicky asked.

"Sometimes."

The librarian held out the photos to Zola. Zola gave a nod of her head to Foster, and the fairy took the photos for his own.

"I appreciate your help in this matter," Zola said. "Now I just need to change this old cloak so I get a few less stares."

✦　　✦　　✦

"WELL THAT WASN'T awkward at all," Foster said as the door clicked closed behind them. "At least she only threatened me with a magazine. That was refreshing."

"Hush," Zola said. "We about gave that poor woman a heart attack. And let's be honest, more than one of us have smacked you."

"I think it was a newspaper last time," Foster said.

"I've never smacked you with a newspaper," Luna said.

"And that's why you're my favorite," Foster said, giving Zola a sly grin. "I'll get these photos to Ward." He tucked them into a pouch on his belt.

"Ward can be a hard man to find," Zola said. "He spent decades learning how to blend in among the Fae. Ah don't know if he'll stand out in Gorias."

"Doesn't matter," Foster said. "He's traveling with the Old Man. If there's one thing Leviticus does well, it's stand out."

"Tell Shiawase hi if he's there," Vicky said.

"I will," Foster said. "Depending on which gateway he arrives at, I may still beat him to Ward."

"Tell me what you learn," Zola said. "And make sure Ward understands how short time is growing."

Foster nodded before he reached out and squeezed Zola's shoulder. He stiffened when Luna wrapped her arms around him, tucking her claws up behind his wings.

"Don't die," the death bat whispered to him.

Foster gave her a lopsided grin. "If I've survived a good whacking from a magazine, I'm sure I can survive Gorias."

"You could take Drake," Vicky said.

Foster nodded as Luna pulled away. "I would. But he's working with Morrigan. Be careful with him, Vicky. He's been playing two sides for far too long. It's easy to lose yourself in that kind of deception."

"I think he was lost for a long time," Vicky said.

Luna turned to face her and Vicky snorted a laugh. Luna looked down at herself and frowned. "I'm shiny."

Foster went to hug Vicky, but she backed away.

"Oh no," she said. "I don't need to be shaking fairy dust out of my hair for the next week."

"Week?" Luna squeaked.

"That's an exaggeration," Foster said, utterly dead-pan.

"How far to the nearest gateway to the Warded Ways?" Zola asked, returning everyone's focus to her.

Foster turned in a slow circle. "Not terribly close. Be nice if Morrigan could pull me back again."

"You could come back to Coldwater with us."

Foster shook his head. "It won't take long to fly out of here. Worst case, I have to get to Louisville. There are a few gateways there."

"So be it. We'll be in Coldwater should you need us."

Foster left as Vicky retrieved the hand of Gaia from her backpack.

"Ah'm glad that library didn't have a metal detector," Zola said, watching Vicky shrug back into the pack.

"Why's that? Oh … right. Guns and bullets and

stuff."

"Yes, child, guns and bullets and *stuff.*"

Vicky frowned at the severed hand. "Fair point. That wouldn't have gone well."

"I suspect not."

They joined hands, and darkness wrapped its cloak around them.

CHAPTER THIRTEEN

G AIA COALESCED BESIDE them, silent for a time before she spoke. "You carry a great power with you. One that was not here before."

"We got the bloodstone," Vicky said, glancing between Zola and Gaia. "We'll be able to move the devil's knot with it. Can I still call on you once we do?"

Gaia pondered the question before nodding. "I believe so. Damian's soul will forever be a part of you. Even should the anchor shift to another, a piece of him will live inside you for all time."

"I hope we can wake you up," Vicky said, looking to the distant shadows as golden pinpricks of light swelled and faded.

"It is no great tragedy should you fail. I will have served my purpose to the last of the mantle bearers."

"Will there never be another?" Zola asked.

"If there is, it will be no concern of mine, being dead."

Zola barked out a quiet laugh at that, but Luna

shrank back, almost hiding behind Vicky. Her discomfort in the Abyss was tangible, and Zola suspected Camazotz had taught her to fear the old Titans.

"Where do we journey?" Gaia asked, her voice ringing around them.

"Back to the cabin," Vicky said. "Coldwater."

They walked in silence for a time, the sudden appearance and fading of the eldritch things trapped in the Abyss almost commonplace now to Zola. And that was a disturbing thought indeed.

A handful of those nightmares unleashed on the world could do damage far beyond Nudd on his worst day. Well, perhaps that was an exaggeration, Zola thought, but he was an insane king with the power to rival most minor gods.

Zola was still studying a towering mass of what appeared to be vines, aside from the fact they were moving, when Gaia spoke again.

"We have arrived. Release my hand and be well."

✦   ✦   ✦

"WHAT NOW?" LUNA asked when they were standing inside the cabin once more.

"Now?" Zola said. "Now we sleep. Or, at least, Ah sleep. You two youngins can do whatever you damn well please."

"That's it?" Luna asked, glancing at Vicky.

"Rest while you can," Zola said. "Once Foster comes back, or Ward, we're going to need to be ready."

"The Burning Lands," Vicky said, lighting a small stack of logs in the stove.

Zola nodded. "The Burning Lands."

Vicky studied the flames as they rose inside the old black stove.

CHAPTER FOURTEEN

FOSTER TOOK A deep breath as the red fires of the Warded Ways faded behind him, and the walls of the golden city of Gorias reached into the blue skies above. He pulled a sash from a leather pouch strapped to his left leg. It wouldn't completely hide his armor, but it was best not to be seen flagrantly displaying the armor of the Demon Sword.

Over the centuries, Gorias had become a battleground between Murias, Finias, and Falias. There were those Fae and traders who wished to travel freely between the cities, but those in power always wanted their share. And when they hadn't gotten it, they'd given rise to madmen like Gwynn Ap Nudd himself.

Foster made his way down the nearest alley. A webwork of them cut erratic paths through Gorias. Cara used to say there were more alleys than streets in the golden city, and she'd had a point. But the alleys were wide enough here for vendors and craftspeople alike to sell their wares.

He never understood why the Lords of Gorias had banished the sellers from the streets themselves. What difference did it make whether you purchased a new blade in the middle of a gilded street, or in the back alley where the afterglow of the golden walls was all the light you had?

Tension kept him rigid and moving at a swift pace, even as the crowds thickened around him. Foster wasn't sure if it was his own need to hurry, or if something darker was propelling him past the stalls carved from stone and magrassnetto.

He caught snippets of conversations, some of the usual bickering between vendors and their patrons, but others were darker, barely whispers of the Mad King's return and the coming conflict with the Lords of Gorias.

Foster slowed at that. He hadn't heard of the lords making ready for war, outside of the fact some quarter of the Fae who lived in the golden city were mercenaries. In that regard, they were always ready for war.

If Ward and the Old Man were recruiting, Foster suspected they'd be hunting for those mercenaries first. Fae who were already willing to fight for coin might be willing to fight for something more. *Trusting* them is where problems arose.

But if he was right, and that's what they were doing, he needed to get to one of the boroughs near the edge of the gates. And not any gates, but those that exited onto the great plains between Gorias and Murias.

Foster spread the sash out around his breastplate as best he could. He didn't know many from Gorias, and only a few he would call his friends. Irontouched and stranger Fae took refuge in the borderlands.

He clenched his teeth, and dove into the shadows.

✦   ✦   ✦

HUNTING OR NOT, Foster eventually gave in to the scents wafting from a strange honeycomb display at the corner of a surprisingly well-lit alley. He was on the outskirts of the mercenary boroughs now.

A rather squat Fae behind the structure, peeked out at Foster. "You're not supposed to be here."

"Excuse me?" Foster asked.

The vendor adjusted the cloak she was wearing, fine lace laid across her shoulders, dark gray filaments tracing the horde of Celtic knots Foster suspected were wards.

"You're from the royal court, yes?" Her voice fell to a whisper. "I recognize you, Demon Sword. This is not a safe place for you. You served on Nudd's court, and there are many here who would see him thrown down."

"I don't serve Nudd," Foster said. He hadn't been to Gorias in a very long time. He had no idea of whether or not the people here even knew Nudd had been responsible for the death of his mother. But perhaps it was time they found out.

"That's not what I've heard," the vendor said. "Heard your entire family was bound to the Mad King. Take what you want and leave. I don't need your kind of trouble here."

"Nudd killed my mother," Foster said to the vendor. "Tell your people that. Tell them how he left her to die in the Burning Lands."

"Ridiculous," the vendor said.

"She did it to save the life of Nudd's pet necromancer."

That gave the vendor pause. "The one who rebelled? Who struck an alliance with the Destroyer? And marched on the very walls of Falias only to vanish?"

That ... wasn't exactly what had happened, but Foster didn't think it wise to correct her. "News travels fast. Things didn't go to Nudd's plan. And a great deal of that is because of the Sanatio's sacrifice. My *mother's* sacrifice. And I will see Nudd burn for it."

"You will find many people here will not be willing

to listen to your story," the vendor said as she pulled a small hexagon of chocolate out of her display. "Take this, for your words. It is not a gift, and you owe me nothing."

Foster took the package, the delicate wax almost feeling sticky in the warmth of his fingers. "The old ways are changing. You can see that. And it is with that in mind that I give you thanks."

The vendor blinked at him, cocked her head to the side, and gave him a small nod.

Foster walked away, slowly peeling the wax seal off the hexagon of chocolate fudge. It wasn't the same here in Faerie, not like Oh Fudge in St. Charles, but this was the stuff of his childhood. This took him back to times that he once thought were better, but which he now understood were a nightmare for so many of their people.

Sweet chocolate melted over his tongue, the honey inside of it bursting into his mouth like one of those awful fruit snacks Vicky liked. But this was far, far tastier. Foster smiled as he ate the rest of it, feeling the warmth that was almost like a vibration seep through every cell of his body.

He didn't think the vendor was misleading him, so instead of continuing on in his Proelium state, Foster snapped into his smaller form. He took to the air, gliding around the narrow finials crowning so many of the buildings in the golden city.

He was closer to the gates now. Foster could make out the enormous bricks and watchtowers that formed the peaks of the city wall facing Murias. A casual observer might not notice the difference in the battlements here, but Foster had been to the walls enough that they were quite obvious to him.

The watchtowers could hold twice as many men, and the iron spikes, dangerous to most Fae, weren't found anywhere else in Gorias. An effective, if brutal way of clearing off anyone attempting to climb the walls.

Of course, that didn't do much good if the fairies were flying. To take care of that, there was a small company of archers manning the wall at all times. Anyone attempting to fly over it instead of crossing through the gates wouldn't live to tell the tale.

The buildings closer to the wall weren't gleaming with the polished gold of the alleys he'd come from. Here the fairies and the buildings both were crowned in dirt and filth. He landed in an area where the neat stalls of the vendors had long since broken down, many abandoned, and others taken over by less savory characters.

But if it was weapons you wanted, weapons that

ERIC R. ASHER

had been proven in battle and quenched in the blood of friends and foes alike, there wasn't a better place in all of Faerie. And where there were weapons, there were mercenaries, and other things that slunk through the shadows.

"Demon Sword."

Foster's steps slowed as he snapped into his larger form. He turned to find an owl knight standing not five feet from him, still armored in the gilded breastplate of Falias, but the metal had been scarred and left to tarnish.

"I'd heard you died, Demon Sword."

"You heard wrong."

"Heard you let Colin die. Your own blood."

Foster narrowed his eyes. This would turn into a brawl if he let it.

"Heard that bitch mother of yours died too." The fairy spat on the ground. "Good riddance to bad rubbish. What kind of Sanatio was she? Walking around with the Mad King's cock in her mouth all the—"

Foster's blade came up through the knight's jaw, cracking through the base of his skull mid-sentence. The fairy tried to grab for Foster's dagger, but Foster ripped it out to a sound that reminded him of a knife slicing through a filet. Foster unsheathed his sword and decapitated the owl knight in two savage blows.

The screams echoed up from the disintegrating body as empty armor clattered to the stone. Foster slammed his blades back into their sheathes.

Something huffed and scratched at the stone behind him. He turned to find a squat black and white bear scowling at him as the sudden silence of the street returned to the normal cacophony of vendors and buyers.

"Happy?" Foster said, frowning at the bear.

The panda chuffed at him.

Foster rankled at the nerve of the panda. "Did you *hear* what he said?"

The bear chuffed again.

"No, I'm quite sure murdering him was *perfectly* reasonable."

Happy growled.

"Use your words," Foster muttered.

The bear's mouth blurred, and the air shook as Shiawase's voice thundered around him. *Follow me.* The booming voice that came from everywhere and nowhere turned a few confused heads, but the now-small fairy riding on the panda's back didn't draw much more than a few cursory glances.

CHAPTER FIFTEEN

H APPY TRUNDLED THROUGH the remains of an old vendor stall, passing into the shadowed archway of a run-down barracks Foster thought looked to be on the verge of collapse. Dust and the scant light from a few windows were all that remained outside of the shattered dark wood remnants of a handful of beds and an armory.

They exited the other side, where two ornate doors stood cracked open, stripped of any precious gems and metals that might have once adorned them. Foster caught some whispers about Happy's presence in the next alley, but nothing that caused him any concern.

Happy stopped in front of a doorway by two pristine vendor stalls. Between them hung an aged gray cup with the words "The Iron Stein" hammered into it.

"Happy?" Foster said from his perch, patting the back of the bear's head.

The panda tossed his head back, nearly dislodging Foster, and snuffled as he pushed through the doors.

Foster didn't miss the warnings etched into that door. They amounted to "Be wary this door unless you be irontouched."

"You trying to get me killed?" Foster whispered as they crossed into the ancient pub.

The few Fae who were inside didn't pay any mind to the panda bumping into almost every chair between him and the far booth. But Foster sure as hell noticed them. They weren't sleek and winged, but instead short and wide and muscled, like they'd spent more years than Mike the Demon swinging a hammer at a forge.

The bartender inclined his head to Foster. Foster didn't miss the iron axes mounted along the hanging racks of steins and glasses. They may have been there for show now, but each dripped with a malice all its own.

Some Fae could die at the mere touch of iron. Others would grow sick over time, but could survive short encounters. But a few, like those who dwelled in that dark bar, and the fairy with the cragged and braided beard in the booth he now stood before, were born immune to its touch.

"Calbach," Foster said.

The Fae offered Foster a smile before taking a long pull from the heavy stein in his hand. "Strange to see you here. I suspect you're not here for me, though."

The dark eyes of Calbach swung to the cloaked figure seated across from him.

Foster hopped onto the table as the man pulled back his hood, revealing the bald head and narrow face beneath it.

"Ward," Foster said. "Where's the Old Man?"

"Recruiting in places I'm not welcome," Ward said. "Which is surprisingly quite a few, considering I saved this place from a basilisk once."

Calbach grunted. "You saved *Falias* from a basilisk."

"And it would have come here if I hadn't!" Ward snapped.

"Pretty words."

Ward's eye twitched. He took a drink from his own stein before calming himself with a deep breath. Ward studied Foster for a time. "What are you doing here?"

Foster hopped onto the bench and drew a thin fabric veil over himself before exploding into his full height, and cursing as his knee thumped against the table. He tossed the fabric over the back of the booth, most of the fairy dust contained.

"Now my shoes are going to glitter," Calbach said. "I liked you better when you just called me to work on the cu siths' lair."

Foster chuckled as he fumbled with the satchel at

his side. He pulled out the photos they'd printed at the library and set them in front of Ward.

Ward frowned at the mosaic. "What is this?"

"A mosaic in the ruins of Falias. It tells a story, much like the pillars on the gates."

"I don't know what you expect me to…" Ward trailed off on the third photo. He started squaring them up until the pattern began to take shape. While Ward studied in silence, and Calbach walked up to the bar for another ale, Foster turned to Happy.

"Why are you still a bear?"

Happy growled at him, and the rest of the bar fell quiet, chairs scooting away from the bear a fraction.

"That's why," Calbach said as he flopped back down onto the bench. "Ghost of a samurai cuts down a Fae, they can process that. Ghost of a panda bear disembowels a fairy and snacks on his innards while he's disintegrating? Bit harder to forget."

"Right then," Foster said, grinning at the panda bear. "Have you found a Ryō coin yet?" He glanced between Happy and Ward.

Happy chuffed.

"It's not just any Ryō coin they need," Ward said, not looking up from the photos. "There were only a handful of smiths forging coins strong enough to host a magic like that."

Happy whined and paced in front of the table.

"Do not despair," Ward said. "I have one secreted away."

"Can we have it?" Foster asked.

"Not today," Ward said. "That would be a bit ... out of the way."

"Do I even want to know?"

Ward frowned. "Probably not. But know that it's safe and no one else can get to it without being dismembered joint by joint."

Foster echoed Ward's frown. "That's ... *very* specific."

"You ever try warding something against Fae who can regenerate their limbs? You need it to *hurt*."

"Now that," Calbach said. "That's the kind of thing Heather was an artist with."

Foster held back on asking Ward anything about Heather. He knew she'd been lost in the battle with Ezekiel years ago, but that had been the last he'd heard.

Calbach shook his head and took another drink. "I'm not having this conversation with you again. Each city is like a different world in Faerie. You should know that well enough by now. You lose one student and it becomes all you can talk about for years."

"I didn't *lose* Heather," Ward snapped. "She made a choice, and it wasn't a choice she could come back from."

Foster thought about asking more about Heather, but instead he asked about the photos.

"You think it's the pattern we need? To move the ..." Foster lowered his voice to a whisper. "To re-anchor the devil's knot?"

Ward shook his head. "I don't think that's a pattern for the devil's knot, Foster. It looks more like a map."

Foster blinked.

"Look here, this spiral, that's almost the exact lay-out of the courtyard and streets where I fought the basilisk in Falias when Ezekiel was running around. The similarity to the devil's knot is a coincidence." He frowned and shifted another photo. "At least, I think it is."

"Wonderful," Calbach muttered. "The basilisk again."

"And this, beneath it, where it squares off a bit more?" Ward said, astutely ignoring Calbach. "I think that's Gettysburg the way it used to be."

Foster cursed under his breath. "If you're right, and this is trailing off to the east, it could lead anywhere."

"I doubt that very much. It leads somewhere the Mad King's been before. You just have to figure out where. I admit though, the similarity to the devil's knot is disconcerting." Ward pulled a small stack of parchment out from a leather satchel at his side. "Let me give you this in case something happens. At least someone will have the pattern needed to try to save Vicky and the others."

"Sure you don't want to go off and die as the only one who knows how to fix it?" Calbach asked.

Ward grinned and shook his head as he traced a series of intricate loops and whorls. Gradually a layered Celtic knot came together, similar to the original devil's knot, but so obviously different that Foster had little doubt it was an entirely different art.

Ward blew on the ink before handing the parchment to Foster.

"What would have happened if we'd used an exact copy of the devil's knot to attempt with the cores?"

"Instead of that?" Ward asked with a nod to the parchment. "Well, that would have been bad. You likely would have killed everyone in a ..." He frowned and squinted a bit. "Hundred mile radius or so? Timewalker magics are overwhelmingly powerful. It's quite possible it could forge a new gateway between the commoners' plane and another."

Foster's eyebrows continued to climb higher as Ward spoke. Apparently, Zola's concern had been very, *very* well placed. "Shit."

The bartender sidled up beside Happy, the bear

nearly reaching the fairy's chest. "For the knight." He slid a ceramic mug toward Foster.

"Why?" Foster asked.

"You're out to kill the Mad King, or so your friends say. And from what I've seen these past weeks, I've no reason to doubt their word."

Foster lifted the mug and took a deep breath. The delicate scent of honey and something sharper wafted from the mug.

"Honey mead. Not the strongest drink on the menu, but one I think you'll appreciate."

Foster nodded to the bartender as he turned to go.

"He's irontouched, right?"

"Most everyone here is," Calbach said.

"I thought they hated all the knights of Faerie."

Calbach harrumphed. "Time changes the most bitter of Fae, Foster. Especially once they see the nightmares of our past being reborn in the realm of the commoners."

Foster sipped the mead. It was sweet, dry, and the flavor blossomed in his mouth. He'd never had finer. "Damn."

Calbach's beard lifted a hair with a cold smile. "Dark times are upon us. Some have seen the omens for many years, but a great deal of Faerie are only now coming to terms with the return of the Mad King." He paused for a short time before holding his stein out. "I am *glad* to have you fighting with us."

Foster cracked his mug against Calbach's and they both drank.

CHAPTER SIXTEEN

WARD MASSAGED HIS temples as Foster got them up to date on the happenings in Falias and Zola's mad plans.

"The good news is we have all three cores," Foster said.

Ward nodded as he gathered up the photos of the mosaic and handed them to Foster. "No need to leave these here where they may be discovered."

Foster tucked them back into the pouch at his side.

"So you mean to make for the Burning Lands?" Calbach asked, scratching Happy behind the ears.

Foster inclined his head. "Mike is there now, scouting things with Sarah. We have the cores for the knot, to save Vicky and Sam, but that's not enough to save Damian."

"And you're sure saving him is the wisest course of action?" Ward asked.

"Of course I am," Foster snapped.

"You know him better than I do. Zola trusts him,

and my trust has long been given to that old necromancer. But there are times when it's easier to let a person go."

"Cara gave her life to save him. That alone should tell you all you need to know."

"The Sanatio was not without a penchant for games," Calbach said. He raised a hand before Foster could protest. "I mean no disrespect by that. But she served long in the courts of Faerie, and no one comes out of that unchanged."

Foster sighed. "No, you're right. But this was different. He was like a son to her. A brother to me. And I have no doubt if it had been up to Damian, he would have died to save her."

"Die to save her, or live to save the child," Ward said. "The choices in this world are shit some days."

Calbach raised his mug to that.

"I'm going back to rejoin the fight in Falias. I need to look at that mosaic again. There may be a clue we missed that's not in the photos."

"We'll send Morrigan what recruits we can. Maybe warn her she'll have a cadre of irontouched on the battlefield?"

Foster barked out a short laugh. "She'll probably love it. Anything unexpected she can throw at Nudd she's going to love."

"We'll get the Ryō coin you need."

Happy chuffed.

"Get it to Zola or Vicky. They're going to need it, and I don't want you showing up in Falias just to die with the coin in your pocket."

Ward tipped his stein to Foster. "Fair enough. One of us will deliver it to them personally."

Foster looked up at the sound of rapid footsteps approaching. His hand flew to the hilt of his sword.

A younger fairy burst through the door, wincing and rubbing his shoulder where the iron on the door had brushed exposed flesh. "Calbach, they're coming!"

The stout Fae chugged the rest of his beer and grinned. Something clicked and chunked and came loose under the table. A battle axe heavier than the beast Mike the Demon wielded rested in Calbach's hands, and the table wobbled with relief.

"Neil?" Foster asked, staring at the wings of his cousin as they spread wide. "What the hell are you doing here?"

"Working with Ward," Neil said as he unsheathed a delicate blade at his waist. "Everyone knows this is the fight to end the king. And where would we rather stand?"

"You should go," Calbach said to Foster. "This isn't a fight you need to join. Too much iron in the blood."

Happy growled and turned toward the front of the building.

"Who are we fighting?" Foster asked as he unsheathed a dagger and a long sword.

Something howled outside as the door rattled in its frame.

"Told you they wouldn't like the silver," the bartender spat.

Foster looked around as the other irontouched took up enormous hammers and iron-banded shields. The door shook again before the frame splintered, iron breaking under the weight of the massive shadow barreling into the pub.

Light seeped into the darkness, and death came screaming.

✦ ✦ ✦

IN THE FIRST moments, as the irontouched unloaded a hammer blow that could have leveled a building, Foster thought it was a werewolf. But this ... this was something else. He'd never seen the like, but he didn't let confusion slow his sword.

"Unseelie shades!" the bartender bellowed as he rushed the nearest of the hulking shadows.

Awe and horror rushed through Foster, tingling down his arms and legs as the pieces fell into place.

These creatures didn't merely move in shadows, they ate the light around them, bringing darkness wherever they walked.

The second irontouched leveled a hammer blow into a shade's gut, but the beast only staggered. It caught the next attack, a reddish glow brightening in the shade's core before a blast of light sent the irontouched to the ground screaming.

Foster lunged, intercepting the follow up swipe with the flat of his blade. Sloppy. He was off his game and he knew it. He hadn't been surprised in a damn long time, but the slender fangs bared at him now, inside his guard, surprised the hell out of him.

He managed to catch the shade with the hilt of his sword, cracking the pommel into the darkness of its body and the glow of its beady red eyes.

The shade twisted violently, backhanding Foster hard enough to send him airborne. Foster's wings snapped taut as he grabbed a stone column in the center of the bar and used the momentum to launch himself back at the shade.

He'd felt the thing's flesh. Fur and muscle and bone. It was time to see if it could bleed.

Foster led with a scream and a low strike with his sword, easily parried by the shade, but it left its neck open. Even as the claws screeched against the steel of his sword, Foster spun, leaving his sword in the shade's grasp while his dagger plunged into the thing's neck.

Blood erupted from the shade as its beady eyes widened. The irontouched regained his feet beside him, only to be run down by a second shade. Foster didn't have to see what happened to know the fairy wasn't getting up again. That kind of gristly crunch didn't end in survival.

"I've got him!" Ward shouted as he slipped behind Foster and the chortling bark of an enraged panda bear drowned the screams of the dying Fae.

Foster didn't turn to watch them engage the other shade. He trusted Ward to a fair degree, but he trusted Happy with his life.

The shade roared, the light-eating essence of the thing fading with the blood rushing from its neck.

"You're not leaving," Foster growled.

For a moment, the beast hesitated, but then the glow returned. The shade raised its arm, silent in the cacophony of the battle around it. Foster knew what was coming next. He launched his dagger after an underhanded feint, catching the shade in the thigh as Foster's right hand found the hilt of the sword abandoned on the ground.

The shade attacked.

Foster had miscalculated. This strike came faster

than the first on the irontouched. A sliver of blue light flashed between him and the shade.

"Are you trying to die!" Ward shouted.

Red and blue crashed together, sending an eruption of sparks and lightning to crash into the open rafters above. As soon as it fell, Foster struck, sword held in two hands as it cleaved through the shade's arm.

It fell away like a shadow, black mist and smoke, but the scream of the beast was real enough.

Black and white wings flashed behind the shade, and its eyes dimmed as a glint of silver slid through its neck, sending the form toppling into two pieces, only to drift away in silence.

Neil stood behind it, his leather armor scorched at the shoulder and a half moon punched through one wing.

Foster turned to find Happy savaging the face of another shade, pieces of the creature falling away as claws and teeth found an ever-deeper purchase. Calbach freed his war hammer, splintering the wood around the spike that had lodged deep inside it.

Ward stood without his cloak, skin bared to reveal the mass of runes and wards etched across his flesh.

"Stop this insanity, Heather," Ward growled.

The shade spoke, only the voice didn't come from the creature itself. It boomed from everywhere and nowhere, not unlike Happy's, but oddly less disturbing.

"You taught me to finish every job. I thought you'd be proud. My offer still stands. Find me and we can talk. Until then, watch your back."

Ward almost growled as he slapped his palm on his upper left pectoral, electric blue light racing around the pattern beneath it and following his fingers as he snapped them out toward the shade.

Four lines of light cut through the shadow, and the creature fell into chunks. Ward clenched his hand into a fist, and the light faded from the patterns on his body even as he pulled a cloak back over the tight muscles of a man who had been in far too many fights.

"Nudd's balls," Calbach spat. "That was my favorite bartender."

A younger irontouched Fae wiped down her war hammer. "Always knew I'd inherit this place one day."

"What?" Neil asked. "Was that your father?" He gestured to the empty armor on the floor.

The fairy blew out a breath. "Hardly. Just the owner. I'm next in line. That's how it goes in these boroughs."

"I'll miss that honey mead," Neil said, casting a longing look at the empty armor on the ground. "Thanks for that, you crochety old bastard."

"I have good news for you on that. I've been making the honey mead for the past century."

"That lying son of a bitch," Neil said, toeing the armor. "And you are?"

"Call me Kat," the irontouched said, reaching out with a broad hand. "You're lucky your friend tips good. If you'd called me barmaid one more time, I would have pulled your tongue out through your neck."

Neil pursed his lips. "Kat it is."

She flashed him a grin before picking up the armor of the previous proprietor. Foster's eyebrows rose as she settled it onto a shelf next to five other breastplates, some showing coats of arms from well before the Mad King's first rule.

Foster took a deep breath and turned to Ward. "What the hell were those?"

"Shades," Ward said. "Somewhat enhanced by a misguided ally."

"Misguided ally," Neil said before he barked out a laugh. "Heather, his apprentice, did it. They had a … falling out of sorts."

Foster cocked an eyebrow.

"She tried to kill me," Ward muttered.

"Deserved?" Foster asked.

Happy released a chortle before he hip checked Ward.

"Shut up, bear." Ward sighed. "I wasn't the most

lenient of teachers."

"The best rarely are," Foster said.

"Regardless, she took small sleights and corrections as personal insults. When the ... *opportunity* arose to seek a different alliance, she took it. I should have spent more time teaching her the ways of the world, and not just focus on the art of warding."

"We all have regrets." Foster said. "You'll be okay here?"

Ward laughed. "Time will tell if any of us will be okay."

"I'll stay with him," Neil said. "Least I can do."

"Least you can do?" Foster asked. "That seems a bit extreme."

"Eh, he saved my drunk ass from a basilisk. It's a favor I promised, and it's a favor I'll repay."

"You gave him a favor while you were drunk, too?" Foster asked, failing to hide the amused smirk on his face.

"Not my best day." Neil shrugged. "But what's done is done, and until *he's* done, I'm staying at his side."

"You should go," Ward said. "You don't need Zola getting impatient and blowing a hole in reality because she doesn't have all the information she needs."

Foster frowned. "That's a fair point." He reached

out and traded grips with Neil. "It's good to see you again, cousin. Don't die before you can regale me with the story of your very bad day."

Neil narrowed his eyes and muttered, "I'll do my best."

"There's a portal in the back if you don't mind a rocky trip," Kat said. "Bit of a hack job, whoever set it up, but it hasn't killed anyone in years."

Foster reached out and scratched Happy behind the ears. "Take care of them, yeah?"

Happy chuffed.

Foster exchanged a nod with Ward and followed Kat to a back room. And by "back" Foster now assumed Kat had meant closet.

She reached into the closet and popped a panel at the back. A jagged, unstable-looking red doorway floated there. He felt like if he went through at the wrong time he might lose a wing.

Kat eyed him, her thick lips pulling up into a small smile. "You might want to be small when you head through."

"I was just thinking the same thing." Foster double checked his pouch for the photos and Ward's drawing before snapping it closed. He took a deep breath, snapped into his smaller form, and glided into the crimson tear.

CHAPTER SEVENTEEN

"**F**UCK," FOSTER SPAT as he stumbled out of the worst trip through the Warded Ways he'd ever experienced. He'd endured spinning before, but this was more like an end over end spiral while someone was beating him in the head with a sparring sword.

He leaned against the bark of the tree beside him and took a few deep breaths in the silence of the woods. Foster ran his tongue over his teeth and checked himself over to see if all his limbs were still intact.

"Fuck."

He looked around the clearing, somewhat relieved to see the small cabin with the green tin roof waiting at the top of a short hill. Of course at that point he wouldn't have been surprised if that trip through the Warded Ways had left him in some kind of alternate hellscape of a reality.

Foster flexed his wings, testing the joints before launching into the air and gliding to the porch. The door was cracked open, so he slipped through without a sound, hearing the refrigerator close as he entered.

"Well, you were right," Foster said as he popped into his full-sized form, spraying the front room of the cabin with fairy dust.

Zola screeched and dropped a bag of frozen chimichangas on the floor. "Goddammit, Ah'm going to have Ward lock this place down tighter than an iron vault." She patted her chest and took a deep breath.

"Sorry," Foster said, doing a terrible job of hiding his grin.

She exhaled slowly and gave him a scowl he imagined Damian had seen on many an occasion. "Now, what was Ah right about, bug?"

"We could have killed everything in a hundred mile radius and punched a hole in reality if we'd used the same pattern for the devil's knot."

"Well shit."

"Do I need to kill something?" Vicky asked as she rubbed her eyes in the doorway to the bedroom.

"No girl," Zola said. "Just get some rest."

A delicate whistle echoed up from behind Vicky. Foster leaned to the side so he could see past her and almost burst into laughter when he saw Luna hanging upside down from the bunk bed. She didn't quite have enough room to hang freely, so her head was cocked at a rather awkward angle.

"Tell me about it," Vicky said, following Foster's gaze. "Her neck's going to be killing her."

Zola punched a few buttons on the microwave and the ancient beast awoke to scour the world of frozen food. "Did Ward have anything useful to say, other than don't break reality?"

Foster opened the pouch at his waist and slid Ward's drawing across the counter. Vicky frowned at the drawing while she ran her fingers over the devil's knot on the back of her neck.

The intricate loops and whorls of the layered Celtic knot in Ward's drawing held all of their attention for a time.

Zola took a deep breath. "Similar, but a different monster entirely. Like the difference between a ghost circle and a circle shield. A complete inversion."

"He said he has a Ryō coin, but it's well guarded. He's bringing it to you. Or Happy is." *Whoever is still alive* was the thought Foster didn't voice out loud.

"Good," Zola said. "Maybe he can help us draw this mess."

"There's more," Foster said, and he told them of the mosaic and how Ward believed it was a map, not a ward.

Zola nodded. "That may be, but there's not enough

here to tell where it leads."

"That's why I'm going back," Foster said. "Morrigan needs to know what's happening, and I want a closer look at the mosaic." He tapped the edge of the last photo. "There could be more, where that filament trails off at the edge."

Vicky picked the photograph up and studied it. Her shoulders sagged. "We're chasing ghosts. Damian's going to die while we're chasing ghosts."

Jasper appeared from underneath the couch, a trail of discombobulated dust bunnies before he pulled himself back into one piece and snuggled up to Vicky's ankles.

Foster didn't miss the sadness on Zola's face as she turned to pull the chimichangas out of the microwave. She took a deep breath and placed a hand over her eyes for a moment. When she looked back to them, there was nothing but steel in the wrinkles on that old face. But Foster could see the moisture hidden at the corners of her eyes.

"First things first, girl. We get that devil's knot re-anchored."

Vicky ran her fingers over the pattern Ward had given them. "No matter what happens. Promise me Gwynn Ap Nudd doesn't get out alive."

Foster didn't hesitate. The price didn't matter anymore. Or perhaps the price had been paid tenfold. "Nudd will die."

"Foster …" Zola started.

"I swear it."

✦   ✦   ✦

LATER THAT EVENING, when Vicky and Luna had passed out again, Zola stood outside the cabin in the ring of stone Aeros had raised, the journal of Philip Pinkerton laid open in her hands.

"What else didn't you tell me, you son of a bitch?"

She closed her eyes when the voice answered. "Anything that might have hurt you."

Zola's teeth cracked together as she turned to face the ghost. Philip Pinkerton stood garbed in a translucent black robe, tied off with a white rope belt. His beard was disheveled, but the moon no longer reflected off his balding head.

"You called and I came, my dear."

"Do you know what this is?" she asked, turning the photos of the mosaic toward him.

He frowned at the images, motioning for her to turn them and shuffle them before shaking his head.

"Damn it all," Zola muttered.

"I would tell you if I knew."

"Would you?" Zola snapped. "Like you told me

you'd freed Ronwe by your own hand?"

Philip threw his hands up in exasperation. "A demon of *knowledge,* Zola. We could have learned everything we needed from her."

"The war was over!" Zola shouted. "You released demons *after* the war!"

"I ... I took things too far."

"As if what we'd done with our own hands hadn't been bad enough, Philip? We could have stayed here. Stayed home. We finally had a *home.* And you gave it up for what?"

"To change the world."

"Bullshit. You gave it up for revenge. *Revenge.* And you didn't even have the courtesy to dig two graves, you bastard. You made me dig yours."

Philip turned away from her at that. "One day you'll understand."

"Oh, Ah under*stand.* Ah'm saying you were *wrong* to do it. To give us a better life ... my god. How did you even lie to yourself like that. You wanted power and revenge."

Philip wheeled around on her. "Revenge that would have made you safe! Made *us* safe!"

"So you forged an alliance with Ezekiel?" Zola pinched the bridge of her nose. "That doesn't matter right now. Do you know where this map leads?"

"I already told you I didn't."

The screen door squeaked behind them. Zola waved her hand through the air, and Philip's ghost dissipated into the ether, wisps of a forgotten life fading to shadow.

"Zola?" Luna asked as she yawned on the back porch. "Who are you talking to?"

Zola stared into the darkness of the woods. "No one." She turned to Luna with a smile on her face. "You want some hot cocoa. Lord knows Ah could use one."

"With marshmallows?"

"Not homemade like that showoff of an innkeeper, but we have marshmallows."

Luna grinned at her.

Zola cast one last look over her shoulder. No one waited among the stones. Only silence and ruin.

Note from Eric R. Asher

Thank you for spending time with the misfits! I'm blown away by the fantastic reader response to this series, and am so grateful to you all. The next book of misadventures is called *The Book of the Rune*, and it's available soon (or maybe now because I'm lazy about updating these things).

If you'd like an email when each new book releases, sign up for my mailing list (www.ericrasher.com). Emails only go out about once per month and your information is closely guarded by hungry cu siths.

If you've enjoyed this book, I would be very grateful if you could take a minute to leave a review on Amazon.

Also, follow me on BookBub (bookbub.com/authors/eric-r-asher), and you'll always get an email for special sales.

The Book of the Rune

The Vesik Series, book #13

By Eric R. Asher

Also by Eric R. Asher

Keep track of Eric's new releases by receiving an email on release day. It's fast and easy to sign up for Eric's mailing list, and you'll also get an ebook copy of the subscriber exclusive anthology, *Whispers of War*.

Go here to get started: www.ericrasher.com

The Steamborn Trilogy:

Steamborn
Steamforged
Steamsworn

The Vesik Series:
(Recommended for Ages 17+)

Days Gone Bad
Wolves and the River of Stone
Winter's Demon
This Broken World
Destroyer Rising
Rattle the Bones
Witch Queen's War
Forgotten Ghosts
The Book of the Ghost
The Book of the Claw
The Book of the Sea

The Book of the Staff
The Book of the Rune*
The Book of the Sails*
The Book of the Wing*
The Book of the Blade*
The Book of the Fang*
The Book of the Reaper*

The Vesik Series Box Sets

Box Set One (Books 1-3)
Box Set Two (Books 4-6)
Box Set Three (Books 7-8)
Box Set Four: The Books of the Dead Part 1 (Coming in 2020)*
Box Set Five: The Books of the Dead Part 2 (Coming in 2020)*

Mason Dixon – Monster Hunter:

Episode One
Episode Two
Episode Three

*Want to receive an email when one of Eric's books releases? Sign up for Eric's mailing list.
www.ericrasher.com

About the Author

Eric is a former bookseller, cellist, and comic seller currently living in Saint Louis, Missouri. A lifelong enthusiast of books, music, toys, and games, he discovered a love for the written word after being dragged to the library by his parents at a young age. When he is not writing, you can usually find him reading, gaming, or buried beneath a small avalanche of Transformers. For more about Eric, see: www. ericrasher.com

Enjoy this book? You can make a big difference.

Reviews are the most powerful tools I have when it comes to getting attention for my books. I don't have a huge marketing budget like some New York publishers, but I have something even better.

A committed and loyal bunch of readers.

Honest reviews help bring my books to the attention of other readers.

If you've enjoyed this book, I would be very grateful if you could take a minute to leave a review. It can be as short as you like. Thank you for spending time with Damian and the misfits.

Connect with Eric R. Asher Online:

Twitter: @ericrasher
Instagram: @ericrasher
Facebook: EricRAsher

www.ericrasher.com
eric@ericrasher.com

Made in the USA
Monee, IL
27 March 2023